Forbitten Fae

A Vampire King, a Fae healer and a betrayal no one could have imagined...

T.W. Pearce

Dedication

Mom, this one is for you.
You always encouraged me to write.
I finally have.
You were taken from this world far too soon and I miss you every day.
Someday, I'll see you on the other side.
Until then, all my love...

Contents

CHAPTER ONE

Hell's Kitchen. Where Demons Dine.

New York City – 1982

Razor-sharp claws and cold fingers of steel wrapped around my throat, cutting off all attempts at air. White fangs flashed as my attacker moved his gaping maw toward my wrist. I groped in vain, desperately trying to push away the vice-like grip while attempting to avoid those 2-inch teeth.

Blood coated every inch of his torso. His chest and stomach had been ripped wide open, and half of his intestines were falling out of his body. His instinct urged him to take my blood to heal himself but getting killed by a vampire was not on my list of things to do today. *This was so not in my job description.*

Eyes watering, I calmed myself as much as possible and laid my hands on the chest of my captor. I blocked out the screaming of the blood servants as they tried to dislodge his choking hands and pin him down.

I centered my magic, shoving it into him. A rush of heat flowed from my palms, and golden light accompanied the gauzy sensation of my magic as it mended his torn flesh. Usually, I send my magic into my patients much more slowly, but the luxury of time was not on my side. It was my life or his—and he was already dead.

As my magic coursed through him and closed his wounds, diminishing the pain and his drink to survive instinct, recognition flashed in his eyes. He immediately retreated, slammed back onto his cot, and looked at me with something akin to horror. He managed to rasp a weak apology before losing consciousness.

My hands reflexively went to my neck as I coughed and tried to suck in much-needed air. I had to heal myself before exhaustion overtook me. I pushed my last bit of energy into mending my crushed throat and frantically gasped in the elusive air my lungs so desperately craved. Just another day in the life of an undercover healer for the vampire seethe.

While vampires' abilities allowed them to regenerate quickly, they required blood to repair their bodies. Usually, that was enough, but when the healing needed to happen more rapidly, they came to their resident fae for help. I was only required when things were serious, and this morning, they'd been quite grave indeed. Not just for the vampires, either—I'd nearly lost my life trying to heal one of them.

Needing a mental and physical break, I walked down three flights of steps in the unassuming building that was the epicenter of the vampire community.

Some species enjoyed showing off or had royalty that lived in more prominent places to make their subjects feel small. However, the vampires seemed fine to live in a building that was not too different than the ones around it, at least on the outside.

Humans build enormous palaces for their royalty, but the king of the vampires preferred to live in an office building rather than some expansive castle. He was a practical man, and his base of operations reflected that.

The vamps had employed me for five years, and I found it easier to go to work when it just seemed like any other building. It helped me forget that I was entering the nest of one of the world's most dangerous beings.

Stepping outside, I inhaled deeply. Then, probably functioning on sheer need more than anything, I made a beeline for the young locust tree on the sidewalk. It was like me, lonely and lacking any companions to share its life with.

Having a relic of the forest was comforting, and I greedily ran my hand through its leaves, just as I did every morning before I entered the building. This small practice always helped soothe my soul and brought me strength. When I use my magic to meld my energy with any type of plant, tree or vegetation, a symbiotic relationship is created. I share a communion with the life I'm linked to and can feel its essence and vitality. I can give and take longevity and healing to and from the greenery.

My daily ritual of exchanging energy with the tree was something I relied on and needed. There were times when my fae home from over a hundred years ago seemed almost forgotten. The flora of earth reminded me of my realm and steadied me for whatever challenges my job brought my way—and it was always challenging.

But I knew the deal when I accepted the position. The Guardians needed someone to infiltrate the vampire seethe and regularly report what was happening behind closed and locked doors. I was eager to prove myself, and this opportunity was the perfect fit for my set of skills.

Training and gifts aside, it was hard to be a fae when your boss was the king of the vampires. Fae and vampires are natural enemies. My fae ancestors were all about life, growth, flourishing energies, and magic. Vampires are the walking dead. We were on the opposite spectrum of life and death, yet here we were.

Still touching the tree, I let my gaze drift across the concrete jungle that was my home. It was a cloudy day, just like all the others. The sun never seemed to reach Hell's Kitchen. It wasn't the most prestigious place at first glance, but it contained all kinds of hidden secrets.

The humans didn't know there were monsters walking among them, waiting to feed on them and orchestrating all kinds of dastardly deeds from the shadows. They didn't realize that whenever they got a paper cut or scraped their knee, someone nearby could smell it.

The vampires had complete and utter control of Hell's Kitchen; it was their sanctuary. Generally, if you weren't one of them, you risked becoming the inevitable next meal.

There was an often-used expression in other parts of the city:

"Hell's Kitchen. Where demons dine."

It was partially correct.

Working for the king of all vampires usually kept me safe from those fangs, which was a definite perk of the job since, to vampires, fae blood was an exquisite delicacy.

Some vampires stared at me a little longer than I preferred, as if they were drooling over my blood. But so far, they hadn't been given a chance to bite me, and I intended to keep it that way.

All in all, the position wasn't as bad as some people would think. To my surprise, I sincerely got along with many vampires in the seethe. The organization's inner circle, the ones I met with the most, were not always kind and welcoming but treated me well enough for an outsider.

The vampires were correct to be wary around me. Fae had abilities that the undead were not accustomed to dealing with. For one thing, they couldn't lie to me. A lie rings much differently in my ear than any other noise; a lie is a sharp, irritating sound, but it is one that I've learned to appreciate since it has saved me many times throughout my long life.

I wished the vampires weren't aware of my built-in polygraph, but they were. Unfortunately, it was common knowledge among supernatural beings. The vampires told the truth whenever possible and danced around a lie when they had to, but they avoided talking to me about any subject that required deceit. It was as amusing as it was frustrating.

Everyone also knew never to thank a fae, or they would be indebted to that fae. Of course, none of them wanted to be in that position. They didn't bother to show gratitude for anything and probably never would, no matter how much help I gave them.

I mentally compiled a report to give the Guardians about the morning's events. I carefully replayed each moment in my mind.

I had barely walked through the door when a familiar vampire came running toward me. Vampires were immortal, powerful beings and did not usually have much reason to rush anywhere. They liked to take their time because they had an infinite amount of it. They only hurried when something was very wrong.

"Moira! Moira!" Elizabeth Fowler was one of the vampires I almost considered a friend—though not quite.

She had been a nurse in her mortal life and continued that practice in her afterlife. "There was an incident last night. We could use your

help! Eight of our guards were attacked and one was killed true dead.
The other seven are in critical condition!"

I didn't hesitate. I jogged behind Elizabeth into the infirmary. It held
ten single beds, with five along each side of the room. Each bed had an
IV to serve blood bags if needed. There were also human blood servants
in the room, ready to offer a vein to anyone who needed a fresh source.

The scene that met me was shocking, at best. Just as Elizabeth had
described, the seven vampires who had survived the attack were suffering
various degrees of nearly mortal wounds. Two of them had neck slashes
so deep that they were nearly decapitated. Four were catatonic, with
wooden stakes protruding from all over their bodies. The last one had
a slashed chest and a massive injury to his abdominal region, with his
intestines spilling from his body.

I immediately went to work on the two who had almost lost their
heads. It took an incredible amount of magic to mend their wounds,
but I patched them up and moved on to the ones who'd been stabbed.
Several other vampire servants had already removed the wooden stakes
from their bodies and poured blood down their throats, so I did not have
to exert as much energy on them. I quickly checked each one, pushed my
magic into them, and then moved to the final victim.

He was the one who nearly killed me. Just like that, my life could have
been snuffed out by a battle-crazed vamp. I could've been gone in the
blink of an eye, with so much life yet to be lived.

Lost in thought, I almost missed the blanched face of a woman
passing by. Her mouth dropped open at the sight of my blood-soaked
clothing. I probably looked like I'd wandered off the set of a horror
movie. I offered a nervous laugh and waved a dismissive hand in her
direction, muttering, "Oh, it's not what you think..." as I turned and
hastened for the door to the building. Was it odd that I felt more

understood in a building full of vampires than I did walking amongst the people on the streets of my city?

Whatever. I had to focus. I needed to find out what happened to those vamps. Whoever or whatever attacked them was incredibly dangerous. The Guardians would want to know if a new superpower was roaming the streets, especially since they were willing to go up against the vampire seethe—something very few were willing or able to do.

Did the Usurpers send this new enemy? The Usurpers were the mortal enemies of the Guardians, and they'd been in a war of good versus evil since 10,000 B.C. The Usurpers' only desire was to eradicate humanity and assume control of the planet. Unfortunately, the Guardians were the only ones strong enough to keep the Usurpers from ruling.

The lynchpin between both factions was the vampires. If the vampire seethe, which was globally strong, decided to ally with either side, it would be a turning point in the war. As an undercover agent for the Guardians, I was tasked with spying and reporting any shifts within the seethe.

Did the vampires know who attacked them? Was this a one-time thing, the start of a turf war, or something much more significant?

There was only one way to find out. I knew I'd soon be paying a visit to one of the most powerful beings to walk the earth: his majesty Sir Adrian Sutton, my boss and the king of all vampires.

CHAPTER TWO

The Vampire King

The crown weighed heavily on Adrian's head—even after centuries. He did his best to lead with clarity and power, but he had to remain ever vigilant. His kingdom would quickly fall into disarray if his people didn't have a resilient ruler to guide them through the unknown.

Adrian had spent hundreds of years building his seethe into something sustainable and robust. He'd taken a ravenous and hostile species and given them order, structure, and peace.

It had required an incredible amount of time and effort to create such a successful seethe, and after all the hardships, he was proud of his accomplishments. At least, for the most part.

It wasn't perfect—nothing was—but he'd managed to keep thousands of vampires safe from the Guardians, the Usurpers, the humans, and the other supernaturals.

All his subjects understood that immortality was not free, and, in some cases, it wasn't immortality at all. They would live forever, but that did not mean they couldn't die. While they were far more durable than the humans they once had been, they were not invulnerable.

Three things could bring true death to a vampire: beheading, the sun, and a wooden stake through the heart. Other weapons—such as silver bullets, various poisons, and a slew of magical spells—could take down a vampire, but they could usually heal on their own if given enough blood and time.

Fortunately, there was a caveat to death by sunlight. Direct exposure would kill most vampires within minutes, but the older ones—the strongest ones, like Adrian—could endure its touch for an extended period. However, if he stayed in the sunlight for too long, the vampire king would end up just as charred as his younger subjects.

As their leader, it was Adrian's job to protect the seethe. Their undeath would last forever if they kept their heads, remained in the shadows, and avoided any pointy sticks. It was easy to do that when they had their own slice of the world to call home, a sanctuary from all other species with which they shared the planet.

Hell's Kitchen might not have seemed like the most obvious choice for their base of operations, but Adrian enjoyed its simplicity. It was not littered with overly large skyscrapers and had just enough other problems to mask their actions in the darkest shadows.

Adrian spun on his heel as he paced, coming face to face with the mirror over his fireplace. He hardly recognized his reflection. His fair skin was paler than usual, and he grabbed a nearby comb when he noticed his hair had collapsed into a mess of chestnut waves after he'd spent an hour carving his fingers through it. Appearance was important to Adrian, and he preferred to look his best at all times. Unfortunately, in his mind, he was always covered in blood. The crimson stains he pictured on his clothing stood in stark contrast to the polished visage he presented to the world.

"You look good. Strong."

His adviser, Royce, stood in the doorway as he usually did when he came to collect Adrian for his duties. Royce didn't look like many vampires. Most were turned during the prime of their lives, but Royce hadn't lost his humanity until he was already past middle age.

His hair was short and gray, now forever on the verge of balding. The creases and age lines he'd developed over his fifty-six years of life hadn't faded away when he became a vampire. His human experience was evident, nowhere more than in his eyes; his icy gaze was filled with a great deal of loss and knowledge.

Adrian knew well what kind of man Royce had been in his mortal life because he had seen it firsthand. He was there when Royce was a British officer, commanding his soldiers into battle.

Back then, the red of their uniforms masked the blood staining the fabric. War was messy, and Adrian regretted getting involved in the one that had raged in the American colonies; however, if he hadn't been a soldier, he would never have met and grown to trust his adviser.

Royce was technically his commanding officer in the British Cavalry at the time, but even then, they both knew who was actually in charge.

Royce discovered the truth about Adrian thanks to a night of poor judgment and carelessness that left Adrian exposed. However, the older man did not flee; Royce wasn't afraid when he saw Adrian's fangs. Those gray eyes grew with wonder at the sight of all the blood and the one responsible for spilling it.

He pleaded to be given that strength, that incredible power, and never relented from trying to prove that he deserved a place among Adrian's ranks. Then, one fateful night, when the enemy's musket ball found its mark and Royce was gasping his final breaths, Adrian finally gave Royce a mouthful of his blood and turned him into the undead man that stood before him.

"I have to look my best," Adrian said. "At least one of those cheeky bastards is going to try to outdo me. They always do." Even after hundreds of years, Adrian's British accent was still evident in his lilting words.

The vampire king's inner circle was known as the Council. They were the ones he trusted most, and they came together once a month to keep everyone in the loop about what was happening within the seethe. Of course, it was irritating to take a break from their daily lives, but Adrian believed it reminded everyone of their allies, their goal, and—most importantly—who they were serving.

He allowed the Council to run their operations as best as they saw fit, but he didn't like the idea of them becoming too self-sufficient.

After all, he was the one who gave them immortality. They owed him a debt for the rest of time, and he expected them to remember that.

Adrian sat behind his desk—his throne, as some of his followers liked to call it—and watched his inner circle start to file into the room. They were all older vampires, some only a few decades younger than himself, and each brought something valuable to the fold. Each member of his Council had earned his implicit trust, but he never allowed himself to grow too comfortable.

It was customary to take precautions.

When each member entered, they opened their palms and let Royce prick their hands with a needle, spilling a few drops of blood into a chalice. Once their blood was collected, Royce downed the liquid in one gulp.

His adviser could taste more in blood than any other vampire that Adrian had ever met. He could taste the thoughts and memories lingering inside one's veins. It was a unique talent amongst their kind and incredibly useful in their line of work. He could identify traitors and rats with just a few drops of blood.

Royce turned to Adrian and nodded, confirming that none of the Council members had thoughts of treason. Royce was more than an adviser and a friend; he was a failsafe that protected them from spies.

With the test out of the way, Adrian began the meeting.

"Good morning, everyone."

Most of the inner circle hated gathering in the morning when the sun was rising. They would have much preferred the safety of nightfall, but Adrian liked to keep them on edge, a reminder that he could endure the sunlight better than most of them.

The meeting proceeded as usual. They went over any developments and updated the group on their business activities. Adrian liked to hear about the progress being made. It had taken him centuries to create a sustainable infrastructure for vampires worldwide. He needed to be confident that the work was being done to his liking.

Felicia Lorne wore beautiful black dresses as if every day of the year was an important event for which she needed to look her best. In addition, she regularly tied her bright, blonde hair back in a tight knot and looked like she had spent hours doing her makeup.

Felicia spoke with an inflated sense of self-importance that she had carried for decades. Since the invention of air travel, she had taken her position of coordinating international affairs much more to heart. There were no long and treacherous sea voyages for her.

Throughout the centuries, Adrian had successfully amassed millions for the seethe, though he never spent egregiously or flaunted his money. The seethe owned many private jets out of a sense of need more than pretentiousness. Those on the Council could travel whenever and wherever necessary without worrying about sunlight, humans, airports, or anything else that may cause vampires to snap and expose themselves.

With how easy it was to get around the globe, Felicia believed she had the world at her fingertips—and sometimes forgot that she wasn't the one in charge.

"Everything from our Asian and African fronts has been going well. It is Europe that occasionally worries me, but we are doing our best to keep it under control. It won't take me long to smooth things over."

As much as Adrian didn't like Felicia's tone, it was the kind of news he wanted to hear. There was always some tension in politics, but if they could get a handle on it quickly, there wasn't cause for concern. The humans hadn't given them much grief since the World Wars.

"I'm sure you will figure it out," Adrian said with a friendly smile. He preferred to treat even his most antagonistic friends with kindness until they lost the privilege. "You always do."

Each of the Council members was centuries old, but as their sire, Adrian had an inherent advantage over them. He was older and more powerful, so a physical contest would likely end poorly for his challenger. He didn't have to worry about that, though. Royce's ability to read the thoughts of those he drank from served as protection against mutiny.

Next up was Augustus Pope, who was responsible for maintaining numbers and recruitment for their organization, dictating who was allowed to become a vampire and who was not.

He was a practical man who prided himself on making the best business decisions. Just as humans had Human Resource departments, Augustus was the head of Vampire Resources.

No vampire, except Adrian himself, was allowed to create another one of their own unless they cleared it with Augustus first, and he was very selective about who he allowed to join them for eternity.

It was a balancing act. The vampires wanted to grow their numbers, but they couldn't draw too much attention. Besides, turning the wrong person could cause a bloody mess for everyone and expose their species to the rest of the world. It was a difficult job, but Adrian trusted Augustus; no one was more scrupulous than him.

Augustus rubbed the dark, gleaming skin of his shaved head and straightened his tie before he read his report to the group. "Our numbers are stable. We haven't made any large increases to our ranks of late. Regarding long-term changes, a senator in Florida who is in our pocket would like to become one of us. We will not grant his request at this time."

"Good call," Adrian said. "I agree. When it comes to politicians, string them along if possible. They will never stop grabbing for power and holding that possibility over his head will make him more complacent."

August nodded. "My thoughts exactly. Besides, there haven't been any major incidents lately that would require us to increase our turnings."

"I'da hold off before'n ya' go an' say that, eh? Just'n case."

Everyone turned to Kellan Fallon, who was leaning back in his seat at the end of the table. Kellan looked the youngest of anyone in the room, but those sky-blue eyes had witnessed over four hundred years of eternal life. The lush, dirty blonde curls under his cap and his babyface created the appearance of a youthful lad, fresh from the green fields of Ireland.

When Adrian stared at him, Kellan removed his cap and twisted it in his hands. His typical carefree demeanor was seemingly hijacked by nervous behavior, which caused more than a few eyebrows in the room to raise.

Adrian didn't like when people were vague and cryptic. "Something the matter, Kellan? Anything we should know that you would like to share?"

"To be honest, sir, I was hopin' that you'da had me speak first so I could get the bad news outta' the way."

"It's a bit too late for that now," Adrian said. "Go on. You obviously have something to say. Speak up."

"Well, it's like this, aye...three of our trucks were hit last night."

That was alarming, but Adrian bit back his immediate concern and stayed focused. There was no reason to get upset until he had all the facts. Adrian leaned back in his chair and turned his body to face Kellan, resting a forearm on his desk. "What trucks? What were they carrying?"

Kellan was usually quick to respond with some cheeky remark. He had been that way since Adrian turned him in Ireland in the 15th century. However, as the silence stretched on, it was clear Kellan didn't want to open his mouth.

"Kellan," Adrian said firmly, not taking his eyes from him. "The cargo. What was it?"

"They were some of our red rigs comin' from the drives."

Adrian's resting hand curled into a fist. Blood. Of course, it was blood.

It was no secret that their kind relied on it to sustain their immortality. Blood was the source of their strength. They needed it, so naturally, someone was trying to take it away.

Decades prior, Adrian had set up a network of hospitals and blood drives to ensure they had a consistent supply of blood. While it might not have been as tasty as the blood that came straight from someone's body, it kept the thirst at bay.

Those deliveries and the surplus of their most crucial commodity kept them balanced and hidden from the human world. It also kept them from making foolish decisions regarding their relations with other supernatural beings.

Adrian kept his composure despite his mounting concern. "If someone is going after our blood flow, they are trying to choke us...starve us even."

"Anyone going after our shipments must know they would be targeted for death the moment they made such a move," Royce said from where he stood against the wall. His pale eyes flickered in the shadows. "No one would dare."

Adrian shrugged one shoulder and gestured in Kellan's direction. "And yet, someone has."

"The Guardians have reason to," Felicia said. "I've heard whispers about them from many of our friends and informants. They still see us as a threat—"

Adrian wasn't so sure. Shaking his head slowly, he said, "We haven't done anything to them. Not directly, at least. I'm sure they've got more important things to worry about than us."

The Guardians were a group of beings that protected humans from the supernatural community. They were not very fond of vampires, but Adrian had done his best not to give them any reason to start trouble.

"Those feckin' Usurpers, then!" Kellan snapped his fingers as if he had just solved a mystery. "They've been wantin' our heads since we did'na join their human hunt, eh?"

That was putting it mildly. The Usurpers were a separate coalition of creatures from a vast quantity of other realms that wanted to eradicate humankind. Adrian agreed that human beings were an inferior species, but he had no intention of extinguishing them.

While some of the conglomerates of the Usurpers could survive without humans, vampires were not the same. Humans were their sustenance, their livestock, and even their potential recruits. They were necessary.

It could have been either the Guardians or the Usurpers. However, Adrian was adamant about keeping his community out of the affairs of either group. He chose to remain a neutral party as they fought each other.

Unfortunately, they had ended up in the crossfire of the two enormous factions. Perhaps one of them was trying to eliminate the vampires while they were unprepared.

It was impossible to tell with how little information they had.

Adrian turned his gaze back to Kellan. "Were any of our shipments salvageable?"

Kellan frowned. "None...and the casualties...they were torn apart. Poor buggers did'na stand a chance. Did ya' see them?"

A jolt of shock pulsed through Adrian. No one had informed him of any casualties, but he kept his expression emotionless, giving nothing away. The last thing he wanted was for the Council to know that he had zero awareness of a critical piece of information under his own roof.

Adrian considered the news. Whoever attacked their trucks had done a thorough job of ensuring last night's blood deliveries were not made.

A vital point needed to be addressed, no matter who was to blame. Ignoring Kellan's question about the wounded men, Adrian asked, "How did they even know where the trucks would be?"

Everyone in the room fell silent. Clearly, no one could answer the question. Even Royce seemed at a loss, and he always had at least one theory; if he did have a guess, he didn't want to share it in front of the others. Neither man missed the hard stares of the Council.

"That's enough for today," Adrian decided. He ended the meeting in the same manner that he always did. "Thank you all for your time and continued efforts toward our cause."

The members of his inner circle filed out of the room one by one, leaving only Adrian and his most trusted adviser. Royce stared at each of their backs as they departed, and then his gray eyes flicked to his superior.

"We both know there is only one way anyone could have known our truck routes."

Adrian nodded. "We have someone on the inside giving away our secrets."

"Precisely. We cannot allow any more information to leak. If any of our multitude of enemies get their hands on more—"

Adrian didn't need to be told that. He cut Royce's sentence short. "I am well aware, and that's why I rely on you and your abilities. You can weed out the ones with ill intentions from those loyal," he said, carefully studying Royce's reaction.

"There are some who can evade my prying mind. Those drops of blood tell me what is on the surface of their thoughts, but I would need to drain much more if I wanted to see further. Still, as much as I would like to believe that my abilities are infallible, magic could shield someone from my sight. Not to mention the ones that can naturally keep me out. But sometimes, the best way to deal with a rat is to crush it beneath your shoe."

Royce never liked to mince words, and his brutal honesty made him a great adviser. His suggestions were based on facts and never involved personal feelings. Of course, it helped that Royce was such a cold and ruthless individual. His icy, gray gaze was constantly assessing his surroundings.

"What would you have me do, Royce?"

"If it were me, I would execute anyone you think might be capable of turning on you. Do your best to ascertain the traitors and make an example of them if you can. The fewer enemies you have, the better—no matter where they originate. Scrub away any potential stains before they grow and become permanent."

"You're suggesting that I potentially harm people that might be innocent...accuse people loyal to me of being traitors."

"Is that something you would be unwilling to do? Sometimes you must make difficult choices to salvage the larger picture. Please consider which members of your inner circle you trust more than others. Which ones do you think could ever betray you?"

Adrian considered Royce. He trusted his adviser more than any other, but also knew that Royce was in the most significant position to betray him. Royce served as his right hand, knowing his weaknesses and strengths. He also was Adrian's gatekeeper, weeding out would-be betrayers. But what if Royce was the Brutus to his Caesar? Royce could easily leak information, lie about a potential mutinous coup, and have access to all confidential details of the day-to-day workings of the seethe.

Royce was suggesting that Adrian randomly execute members of the Council without provocation. Could he be behind the leak? Did he want to assume power for himself or another? If so, removing Council members made sense, as they could challenge Royce or Royce's new liege for the ruling position.

But why would Royce suddenly turn on him after centuries? What would he gain by betraying his king, the one to whom he'd always been intensely loyal? Adrian wrangled his warring thoughts and focused on the conversation at hand.

"I'm not one to give in to paranoia."

"No," Royce said with a humorless little laugh. "But, thankfully for you, I am not afraid to seem paranoid. Being overly cautious could save everything we've built."

"And acting too rashly could destroy everything anyway."

There was a knock on the door, and their tense conversation abruptly ended. Still, Adrian could feel Royce's icy stare boring into him as he turned away from his adviser to look toward the door.

Both men knew who stood on the other side. The combined scent of rich soil, moss, and fallen pine needles touched by morning dew were unmistakable, and only one smelled like that.

Adrian's expression softened as he said, "Come in."

"Sorry...I hope I'm not interrupting?"

The woman that stepped into the doorway looked at the two men with some uncertainty. Nevertheless, she walked with graceful confidence as she moved through the room and stopped in front of Adrian's desk.

Adrian was startled but hid it well as he took in her appearance. The ugly tableau of blood staining her clothing starkly contrasted with her beautiful face and long, red hair. She was ghostly pale and her movements were sluggish. Her eyes showed a weariness that was not typically there, indicating her level of exhaustion.

It was Moira Collins, one of the few people in the building who wasn't a vampire. Instead, Moira was a fae, powerful in her own right but in a very different way to Adrian and his brethren. While their power came from the life force they consumed, her power was life itself.

The magic she used took its toll on her. He had seen her pass out from the strain of healing his soldiers. Remembering Kellan's description of the injured men, he glanced at Royce and made a mental note to uncover why no one informed him about the attacks.

He returned his attention to Moira. It was apparent that she had severely drained herself by healing his men.

"No, you're not interrupting. Of course not, Moira," Adrian said, suddenly feeling very agitated at her disturbing appearance. He turned back to his adviser, whose grave expression was laced with annoyance. "Royce was just leaving anyway."

Some vampires in Adrian's inner circle were weary of having a fae so close. Royce was one of her most vocal detractors; he didn't like that he couldn't read Moira's thoughts like he could read the minds of others. He was accustomed to being able to pry, and the man trusted no one.

"Yes, I must be going...I am sure we will have much more to discuss later."

That was Royce's way of promising that their conversation wasn't over, and all Adrian had done was delay it. With that, the adviser walked past Moira, sighing in agitation as he glanced back at the vampire king and the fae healer. The door handle offered a soft click as Royce pulled it shut behind him.

With Royce finally gone, Adrian rushed around his desk to stand beside his healer. He placed a hand on her shoulder and urged her to sit in one of the Victorian-style chairs that adorned his office. Then, using his vamp speed, he flashed over to the antique hutch that held coffee and tea decanters.

He quickly poured steaming black tea into a wine-red mug, added a generous amount of fresh cream, and then dropped in six sugar cubes, stirring it all with a silver spoon. Next, he placed the tea on a matching saucer and, using tongs, selected three chocolate-covered tea biscuits from a porcelain bowl and added them to the plate. In a blur, he was standing next to Moira again, offering her the tea and cookies.

"You look as if you've had a rough morning. Please, eat and drink. You could probably use the sugar."

Moira blushed, accepting his offerings as she thanked him.

The only sound in the room was the soft crunching as she ate, dipping the biscuits into her tea. Adrian couldn't pull his eyes from Moira's throat, watching in fascination as she swallowed each bite and drank the hot, sweet liquid. He felt strangely pleased that he was providing sustenance and caring for her.

Throughout his long life, Adrian had known many healers. He'd encountered mages, druids, shaman, witches, and warlocks. He'd employed hundreds of healers worldwide, yet he had never met someone as gifted as Moira.

He'd once witnessed her bring a human back from the dead. Two years prior, a young vampire Adrian had just turned could not handle his bloodlust, and he went rogue, slaughtering a 12-year-old child.

The blood of children was ambrosia to a newly turned vampire. Adrian had a strict no-children rule in place in the seethe, so the boy wasn't even supposed to be there, but one of the blood servants had brought her son into the building because he had a fever and could not go to school that day. She'd only intended to pop in for a minute to grab something she'd left in the building, but that horrible decision changed her life forever.

It happened so fast. Adrian was down the hall when he heard the scream and the guttural sound of the rogue vampire tearing into the boy's throat. Adrian was in the room in a blink. He quickly killed the rogue, who was so full of bloodlust that he did not even notice his king.

Adrian scooped up the boy, flashing at vamp speed toward Moira. But he was too late. As he rounded the corner into the infirmary, he heard the final, fluttering beat of the little one's heart.

Eyes wide with horror, Moira flew across the room to meet Adrian, and although the child's life had already left his body, she touched him, thrusting golden light into his tiny corpse. Within seconds, the child's throat mended, and Adrian heard his small heart start up.

Adrian had never admitted it to anyone, but that experience was something he would never forget. When Moira sent her light into the child, she was so frantic to save him that she used far more magic than ever before, and unwittingly, some of it transferred into Adrian. It was the single best thing he'd ever felt in his undead life.

It felt like the sun was shining inside his body, bathing him from the inside out and surrounding him with a warm, all-encompassing shield of safety and strength.

For the briefest moment, for a whisper in time, Adrian was alive again—truly alive. Then, in sync with the tiny, frail boy he held in his arms, Adrian's black heart began beating after 600 years of sitting silently inside his chest.

Adrian staggered under the feel of it, the presence of life inside him. His shock was quickly trumped by absolute joy and pure, unadulterated light. He remembered what it felt like to be human, with all its wonderful and horrible fragility, and then, just as quickly as his heart had started, it stopped, plunging him back into the same black existence he'd dwelled in for centuries.

He'd thought a thousand times about that day with Moira, about how her magic felt inside him and how his soul was as clean and innocent as a newborn babe for one tiny moment. He'd thought about how much he would give to experience it again, to feel alive again, but that was not his destiny. No. He was the vampire king, not some foolish boy chasing the dream of a girl. It did not matter that Moira had given him the one thing that all vampires longed for—hope.

Adrian knew he could never tell anyone about that day. First, it would give Moira power over him, and second, it would make her a target. If others found out that she possessed the ability to, even briefly, bring them to life again, she would become nothing more than a highly sought-after drug for most vampires. No. Moira Collins was his, and he would protect her.

Swallowing the last of her tea and resting the dishes in her lap, Moira said, "I don't know why he hates me so much. Do you know that I've never seen him smile?"

Still lost in thought, Adrian was momentarily confused. "Oh, you mean Royce? I'm not sure that he's capable of that," he said with a snicker, leaning casually on the front of his desk with his hands in his pockets. "Royce doesn't like to express himself...well, sometimes. He has no problem telling me when I've done something wrong. But he means well enough."

Adrian gestured for the cup and saucer, placing them on the corner of his desk as Moira nodded her thanks.

"I'll take your word for it. It's not like we talk to each other anyway. Royce does his best to pretend that I don't exist." Moira sighed.

Adrian smiled at her. "Don't take it personally. He pretends most people don't exist. He's an old codger, that one."

"Aren't you older than him?"

"Is that a roundabout way of asking my age?" Adrian said with a wink. It was an interesting question, and he understood her curiosity. "Technically, I suppose, but his mortal life was longer than mine."

"Is that how vampire ages work?"

"It is a never-ending debate in our community. But we can talk about that another time." He made a point of looking directly at the blood on her clothing. "What brings you to my office this morning?"

"It's about what happened this morning. I wanted to update you on your soldiers' progress. I mended their wounds and they're all sipping on blood to ensure they're back to full strength. But..." she hesitated and looked down, rolling the fabric of her jeans between her thumb and forefinger.

"But?" Adrian followed up.

Her eyes met his. "It's just that those men, all seven of them, were nearly truly dead. So, whoever or whatever attacked them took down seven of your most accomplished soldiers and managed to kill one true dead. I've never seen anything like it." Moira's concern furrowed her brow. "Do you have any idea what attacked them?"

Adrian considered her for a long moment. It was unlike her to ask specific questions about the wounds she treated.

He must have hesitated for too long because she continued, "The only reason I ask is that I'm assuming the trucks were hit close to home, inside Hell's Kitchen." Adrian's brows raised at this conclusion, and Moira noticed his hands left his pockets, and he folded his arms across his chest.

"Their injuries were so severe that there is no way they would have survived unless they were very close by when they were attacked. Even I would not have been able to save them if they had a long distance to travel to receive healing, especially in New York traffic. So, if there is something out there, something strong enough to take down eight vampire warriors at once, and it is that close...." Moira stopped, shook her head, and looked at him imploringly with those large, blue-green eyes.

"Then how are any of us safe, eh?" Adrian asked.

Moira slowly nodded, her gaze never leaving his.

"Moira, I don't want you to worry about this. You are safe within these walls, and you will be safe inside Hell's Kitchen."

"But how can you guarantee that?" she countered, surprising Adrian. "Those soldiers weren't safe, and Dustin is on the streets every night. We walk to and from work together. If someone out there is gunning for you and knows that we work for you, then...." Moira opened her hands, palms facing up as she shrugged.

"Right, then." Adrian stood straight, dropped his arms to his sides, and briskly walked around his desk to sit in his chair. "You needn't question my ability to keep my people, including you and your husband, safe. My enforcers are working on this as we speak, and I'm confident they will have the situation in hand shortly."

Dustin. Adrian often forgot that Moira was married and to someone that worked for him, no less. Dustin Collins had been a capable enforcer of his, collecting tributes for the vampires despite being a shifter himself. Shifters were robust and adaptable creatures which made him a great asset, especially when he needed someone to go into shifter territories, which vampires could not enter without serious political complications. Outside of his usefulness, though, Adrian wasn't a big fan of Dustin. He wasn't the friendliest of individuals, at least not toward him and his kind.

Maybe Dustin didn't like that he would sometimes be asked to help traffic other shifters instead of collecting tributes. But it wasn't anything personal and even if it was, Adrian was well within his rights to ask that of him.

Moira and Dustin didn't seem very close. There was an awkwardness between them whenever they were together, and Adrian wondered how they could be married. Their lack of chemistry was almost painful to witness.

"I'm sorry, I didn't mean to...." Adrian put his hand up, cutting her off mid-sentence. He glanced at her bloody shirt again, and his eyes softened.

"Don't give it another thought. I understand you are shaken from this morning's rush of injuries, and I..." he almost thanked her but stopped himself. He knew better than to thank a fae. As much as he admired Moira, he didn't want to be in her debt. "You did well, as always. I can see that just from how tired you look. It must have taken a lot of your strength to heal them. I insist you take some time this afternoon to rest. Make sure you eat, change those clothes, and take a long nap to rejuvenate."

"I'll be okay," Moira said. "I'll ask Dustin to run me a hot bath and maybe give me a massage later tonight. That usually does the trick."

Adrian flattened his lips at the thought of her naked with Dustin. But, instead of dwelling on that thought, he shifted gears, "Do you think I am putting too much pressure on your husband? On the contrary, I would like to think that I keep him busy and that he finds satisfaction in his position. But, of course, I know that you keep him happy, first and foremost."

Moira studied him. "Dustin handles pressure very well, and I know he prefers to keep busy. Fortunately, his cheetah nature demands the hunt and the anticipation of besting his prey, so the work is good for him." She stared ahead at nothing as if lost in thought. "And as for me keeping him happy...I hope so," Moira said. "I do my best."

Adrian smiled. "I'm sure that your best is enough.

CHAPTER THREE

The Favor

"**Y**ou weren't at this morning's meeting."

"Are you surprised?"

Bastien Champagne hadn't been to a meeting in decades despite being one of Adrian's closest allies. While many other old vampires he worked with stayed in Adrian's immediate vicinity, Bastien had other ventures that consumed his time.

He was a world-renowned chef who owned twenty-four prestigious steakhouse restaurants all over the globe. While most of those restaurants catered to high-end customers, the Belfry in Hell's Kitchen was reserved for a very exclusive clientele. It was a haven for vampires because the chef's cooked meals with specialized flavoring and sauces, pleasing even the most discerning palates.

Bastien was turned during Adrian's travels to New Orleans back in the 1800s after promising he would continue to cook for him for eternity.

Over the last two centuries, he cooked his way from the bayous of Louisiana to the world stage, creating a culinary empire—though the emperor of food was still loyal to Adrian as his king.

He still wore his dirty blonde hair in a knot at the base of his skull to expose his handsome features. His confident smirk showed amid an exact amount of stubble on his jaw.

"Why would I attend one of those boring conferences when you and I can discuss the same topics over a warm meal? It's so much more pleasant and not nearly as crowded, no? I don't have to wait for my turn to speak and listen to all the others trying to prove their worth. I know mine." Bastien's ego was as large as his personality.

"Sometimes, being a team player is not all bad."

Bastien ignored him. He cut into his steak and speared a piece with his fork. The meat was nearly raw and dripped with blood. Before taking a bite, he let it hang in the air for a moment. "Rumor on the street is that some of your red rigs got hit, eh?"

Adrian glanced around the restaurant. It was darkly lit and windowless to keep out the sunlight. It was always crowded with vampires enjoying a relaxing meal. All the people around him were too focused on their food to be eavesdropping. At least, he hoped.

Turning his attention back to Bastien, he looked at his old friend through narrowed eyes. "Where'd you hear that?"

"People like to talk while they eat." Bastien chomped down on the beef and flashed an arrogant grin with the meat between his teeth. "See? I don't need to attend meetings to know what's happening."

"That's why you are the best at what you do." It was true. Not much happened in Hell's Kitchen—or anywhere else—that Bastien didn't know about. He had eyes and ears all over his restaurants, listening to every conversation.

Besides being a chef, Bastien was quite adept at gathering knowledge. He served information to those willing to pay, but only if the information was sufficient to share.

"So, you got any suspects so far?"

"Not yet," Adrian said honestly. "But we're working on it. I was hoping you could keep a few ears out."

"For you? Mr. Royalty himself? I always do, free of charge, my friend. Free of charge. You didn't have to come all this way to ask me a thing like that."

"That's not all," Adrian said, knowing the next request wouldn't be as simple. "With our red rigs down, we require a bit of extra blood."

Bastien nearly choked on his food. He washed it down with a glass of blood, ensuring he drank every drop before loudly placing the empty glass between them on the table.

"And you would like me to hand some of my supply over."

"It's common knowledge that you have a surplus you use for your prep."

"I keep our kitchens well stocked, yes, but handing over what we have will hurt our—"

"We will compensate you," Adrian said, cutting him off. "Please understand that this isn't a request."

For a moment, Bastien's expression darkened. He was a mighty figure in the city, in both the vampire community and other circles, but his popularity and status did not outshine Adrian's throne. He knew there was nothing he could do but obey. He bit back his defiance, cracking his neck before suddenly flashing that signature sideways grin.

"Of course. Anything for you, my friend, anything at all. I am always ready to serve whether it's breakfast, lunch, or dinner."

That was what Adrian liked to hear.

Still, Bastien couldn't help himself from requesting an alternative. "Why not continue the human trafficking circuit you used to do? Squeeze some of them dry for their fresher stuff?"

The thought had crossed Adrian's mind, but he dismissed it. "I'm trying not to get on the Guardians' bad side right now, and if humans begin disappearing in large numbers, it might draw unwanted attention."

"I get that," Bastien said, relenting. "Fair enough. I will provide you with whatever you need, my king," he quipped, accentuating his agreement with a head bow and flamboyant flourish of his hand.

Adrian smiled, but it did not reach his eyes. Bastien's mocking gesture was not lost on him, but the chef was a known showman, so Adrian knew not to take his sarcasm to heart. He was satisfied for the moment. Replenishing their blood supply after the loss of those trucks would at least alleviate some of the stress permeating the vampire community.

Borrowing extra blood was not a permanent solution, merely a bandage over a bullet wound. The only way he could stop the bleeding was to determine who was responsible for hitting his trucks—and, more importantly, finding the rat who sold them out.

CHAPTER FOUR

The Husband

Dustin Collins didn't look pleased to be there, he hardly ever did. He was still uncomfortable around vampires, even after years of working with them. Dustin was a shifter, able to transform his body into a cheetah. He could also do a partial shift, only transforming enough to use his claws and fangs, while remaining in mostly human form.

Adrian wasn't his biggest fan, but Dustin was a competent worker under his employ. He was great at collecting tributes and even though he hated it, Dustin was good at transporting other shifters, too.

There was a lucrative industry of shifter trade for all kinds of reasons. The best person to catch shifters was another shifter. He used that cheetah speed of his to abduct his fellow creatures.

"How is the hunt, Dustin?"

"Same as always," he said unenthusiastically.

Adrian glanced at the clock. "You're late again."

"Sorry. The wife and I were in the middle of an important conversation. Lost track of time."

Once again, Adrian could not resist prying into Dustin and Moira's marriage. It was just too tempting.

"Yes, Moira had a challenging morning. How is she feeling now?"

Dustin raised a brow and stared at him like he was trying to ascertain if his concern was sincere. His answer was hollow and challenging to read. "She's fine."

"Good to hear," Adrian said. "Moira has been great and has proven herself invaluable. I hope she took some time to rest this afternoon."

"I said *my* wife is fine," Dustin growled. His upper lip curled as he met Adrian's gaze with a steely look.

Adrian, king of the vampires, was nothing if not an alpha male. He felt his dominance rise within him at the challenge in Dustin's body language.

Dustin realized his momentary lapse in respect and dropped his eyes from Adrian's, focusing on his desk instead. "Thank you for asking; she did rest," he finally said, taking a visible step backward. "And yes, Moira's amazing."

"Indeed." Adrian checked his aggression, and since he had no desire to draw out the conversation with Dustin, he decided to get directly to business. Luckily, he had something in mind that would pique the shifter's interest and quell the testosterone in the room. "I have a new hunt for you...and this one won't be like your others."

Dustin's eyes flicked to Adrian's as he raised his brows, but he held his tongue and quickly looked at the desk again.

"We won't send you after tax evaders or your fellow shifters, so you'll get a break from going after your kind. Well, possibly. It depends. Someone attacked a few of our red rigs carrying a great deal of blood. I want you to hunt down those responsible and bring them to me."

The shifter cocked his head to the side and narrowed his eyes. "You would trust me to do that?"

Adrian studied him for a minute. "Is there a reason I shouldn't trust you?" A challenging half-smile lingered on his face, but before Dustin could offer an answer, he continued, "We will all be looking, but you can go places that we cannot."

Outside of Hell's Kitchen, vampires were largely rejected from society. Some parts of the city were antagonistic toward them, and they usually did not dare to venture into those areas as they risked an attack. In addition, there were feuds and grudges in some neighborhoods that were unresolved.

"I will do my best," Dustin said with some uncertainty, rubbing the nape of his neck under Adrian's intense stare.

Adrian did not wholly trust his shifter enforcer, but he was desperate to discover who attacked his trucks sooner rather than later. Having another set of eyes on the case would be helpful.

"Brilliant." Adrian nodded and gestured toward the door. Dustin stood from his chair, turned, and took a few long strides for the exit.

"Right then. Happy hunting and please say hello to Moira for me."

Dustin stopped in the doorway and glanced at Adrian, who noticed the barest quiver of his top lip. He looked like he wanted to snarl at Adrian, but instead, he gave a stiff nod.

CHAPTER FIVE

A Little Boring

T he rest of the day was uneventful. There was no news of the culprits and Bastien Champagne didn't call with any information. Dustin Collins failed to return with a prisoner and none of Adrian's other grunts on the ground reported anything, either. It was a quiet day in Hell's Kitchen, and Adrian grew nervous as nightfall approached. More trucks were likely to be hit.

As the sun began to set, Adrian walked by Moira's office. He noticed her packing her things to go home for the night. She smiled in his direction, and he paused, caught in the hypnotic pull of her attention. He regretted his response to her earlier concerns—his jealousy and dismissal of her fears clawed at him.

Ducking into her office, he asked, "Do you mind staying?" He needed someone to distract him. His conflicting emotions and thoughts were burying him. The attack on their blood supply had rattled him, but he couldn't let anyone see his concern—at least, he couldn't let his fellow vampires see. But Moira was different.

While his uncertainty would be perceived as weakness by the members of his inner circle, he knew that Moira wouldn't see it as such. She understood the danger he was facing, perhaps more than anyone, because she had treated the wounded men. The gravity of their situation weighed heavily on his mind, and he realized that he should have acknowledged her fears earlier instead of allowing his pride to be affected. Moreover, he knew from past conversations that Moira often gave better advice than Royce, the man appointed to the job.

Moira brushed some of her long red hair out of her face and glanced at the clock on the wall, probably thinking about her husband since he usually walked her home at night.

"I don't mind," she finally said, and he hoped that was true. "But only if I can ask you something." She smiled coyly like she was proud to be bartering with him.

Adrian accepted her terms. He leaned his right shoulder against the door frame and took the weight off his right foot, cradling it behind his left one. He crossed his arms over his chest and repeated what she had said to him. "I don't mind."

Moira made her way to the doorway, stopping in front of him. "Do you enjoy being king?"

That was not a question he thought about often. He didn't have the luxury of considering whether he liked his position or not because his enthusiasm for the role made no difference. He didn't have to enjoy it; he just had to be good at it, or their whole species would be at risk.

Eyes narrowing, he said, "That's a tough one. A complicated one, really. And I haven't given it much thought."

"You must have before."

"Not especially. I never saw much point in dwelling on something like that. But, whether I like what I do, it is a job I must do. I spent centuries building my kingdom. I am certain that without the infrastructure of the seethe, vampires would not be nearly as strong as they are today. I suppose I enjoy knowing that it has all been worth it and that I've made a difference for my people."

"You strike me as someone who doesn't enjoy having so much power and responsibility. I've met egomaniacs, and you don't seem like one of them."

"Oh, I don't? That's a relief to hear. I hope I am a better ruler than many others who have had to wear a crown in this world."

"I think you are," Moira said. "You haven't given me any reason to think otherwise. You're a little boring, if anything."

Adrian felt like he'd been slapped in the face. "Boring?"

Facetiously, Moira said, "Oh yeah," as she waved a dismissive hand toward him. "You just stay in the dark all day and boss people around at night."

People did not tease the vampire king. If someone else had said something like that to him, he might have torn out their tongue, but when she said it, it made him laugh.

"I'm just saying you need a hobby, that's all," Moira said. "You lived during the time of some famous painters, right? So why not take up painting?"

"No one wants to see my art, believe me," he said, grimacing. "But I have hobbies."

Now it was Moira's turn to fold her arms over her chest as she flashed a grin and leaned forward. "Really?" she said, drawing out the word. "Name one."

Adrian wasn't accustomed to being challenged, and the intrigue of it thrilled him. He had lived a long time and had plenty of secrets, but there were harmless things he kept from most people, small things that brought him joy over his many decades and lifetimes.

Maybe it was time to let someone else in on one of his secrets. At the very least, it would silence Moira's claim that he had no hobbies when that was not the case.

Adrian bowed toward Moira until they practically touched noses. Then, conspiratorially, he whispered as if he was bringing her in on something confidential. "I want to show you something."

CHAPTER SIX

His Hobby

"I want to show you something."

Six simple words. Six words should not have sent a zing through my body, but they did. No one with eyes could deny how beautiful the man—well, vampire—was. His thick brown hair, perfect features, eternal five-o'clock shadow, and excellent build were impossible to miss.

But still, what was wrong with me? First, vampires were the enemy. Second, I was married; even though it was a fake marriage orchestrated by the Guardians as part of my deep cover, it was not appropriate to go off alone with another male. Third, and most importantly, I was on a mission. I had a job to do as a Guardian.

Then again, I could use his invitation to my advantage. The playful banter was working in my favor since Adrian asked me to stay and clearly had an agenda. My imagination might have taken a bit of a deviant turn while processing his last statement, but Adrian Sutton was not a 15-year-old boy. I had asked him to name a hobby, but he didn't want to speak it aloud. Apparently, it needed to be seen to be believed.

He seemed nervous and the undisputed vampire ruler in all his undead glory, didn't get nervous. Even so, his pale face grew red, and he gestured for me to follow him.

I marched after him, curious to see where this would lead. I was the one that wanted him to share a hobby, after all.

We entered the stairwell and started to ascend the seven floors of the building. Why Adrian opted for the stairs instead of the elevator, I didn't know. Maybe he didn't want to encounter others in the building, and the elevator was always busy.

Adrian's finely pressed white button-down shirt hugged his lean, muscled back, and as he climbed the stairs in front of me, I had a perfect view of his black slacks, which accentuated his firm bottom. The man had a beautiful backside, there was no doubt about it. Focus.

Adrian was remarkably quiet during the climb, but he occasionally glanced back like he was making sure I was still following. He seemed surprised to find me there each time he peered over his shoulder.

When we reached the top of the stairwell, he paused in front of the door to the roof.

Adrian let out a long sigh, like he had been holding his breath the entire way up, and flashed an awkward, sideways smile at me. It was cute but undeniably alarming since he wasn't the kind of guy to lack confidence.

"What you are about to see is one of my best-kept secrets. It is not something I share with anyone, and I would like to keep it that way. So, Moira Collins, I will have to swear you to secrecy."

Now I had to know.

"Come on. Swear that you won't tell anyone."

I remained silent to torment him a little. It was rare to hold any power over the king of the vampires. I put my hand to my chin, squinting my eyes as if I had to really think about it, but I couldn't tease him too much, not when he looked so concerned and regretful.

"Out with it," he said with another nervous chuckle as he made a forward motion with his hand. "Don't make me beg."

"Fine!" I made sure to smile just to put his mind at ease. "I won't tell anyone about...whatever it is you are about to show me." Adrian waited for a vow, so I finally gave him one. "Okay, okay! I swear it. Happy?"

Adrian remained uncertain, staring at me for a long moment. It was hard to look away from those deep pools of brown, which seemed to see far more than I wished to reveal. Finally, Adrian nodded as he slipped a key into the door, unlocking it and pushing it open.

I didn't know what I was expecting—but it wasn't what I found.

The rooftop was its own miniature forest. I gasped as my delighted senses greedily drank in the foliage. There were plants and small trees, and there was even a built-in koi pond with a meandering stream trickling over river rocks coated with algae. Boulders with green moss were carefully positioned throughout, offering natural places to sit and take in the colorful flowers as they danced in the evening breeze. Home. This was home to me—or it was as close as a forest fae could get in the middle of a concrete jungle.

My hands covered my mouth and tears of elation welled in my eyes. "Adrian!"

His name was barely a whisper on my lips, but Adrian stopped his progression through the greenery and whirled to look at me. He still looked quite nervous, but a smile appeared when he took in my reaction.

I lost myself in that moment, in the scene before me, in the night, and in my wonderment of the man who had created such an implausible likeness of my home realm on a rooftop in New York City.

Who was Adrian Sutton? How could one be so paradoxical? I knew he was capable of great wrongs and horrors. Before I accepted my current undercover position, the Guardians had informed me of Adrian's crimes. They wanted me to have a clear understanding of who I would be working for. Adrian had been involved in a myriad of illegal activities and a considerable amount of innocent blood stained his hands. Yet those actions were contradicted by the tenderness and care he obviously showed the vegetation that surrounded us. I thought about the tea and cookies he had rushed to provide me in his office and considered the genuine concern he'd exhibited—at least until I'd mentioned Dustin.

Crap. Dustin.

Thinking of Dustin forced me back to reality. I remembered who I was and, more importantly, who Adrian was. I cleared my throat and straightened as I casually said, "I didn't realize you were a botanist."

He shrugged his shoulders uncomfortably. "Well, I wouldn't go that far. But I have always had a fascination with plants." He gently touched a nearby forest pansy, admiring its purple leaves. "It's just nice to look at them sometimes. Their lives are so fragile and fleeting, and to hold that kind of mortality in my hand," he trailed off. "I guess there's a comfort to it."

He had a point. A vampire lived in a perpetual state of undeath. That kind of existence no doubt made little flickers of real, temporary life fascinating for them. They could never have that again after they lost their mortality.

"I collected most of these from different parts of the world."

"Now you're just bragging," I said with a laugh. "No one likes a show-off."

As beautiful as the collection of plants was, I couldn't help but notice their wilting leaves and dull colors. The vampire king no doubt did his best with his limited time and with their placement. Though the rooftop was large, some of the vegetation lacked the space it needed to spread. Some species of plants were loners and could not flourish properly, if overcrowded.

Nevertheless, Adrian had done an impressive job building a foundation of deep, rich soil, and I noticed an irrigation system that stemmed from the koi pond, feeding all the vegetation.

Despite his efforts, some of those plants weren't meant to thrive in a place like Hell's Kitchen.

"They could do with some more sun."

Adrian raised a brow. "Is that supposed to be some kind of vampire joke?"

"It's just the truth."

I held the petal of a nearby moonflower between two of my fingers. The plant was weak—I could feel that much just from touching it. It needed to be coaxed and pushed forward, rejuvenated. My magic could boost its latent potential. I lowered my fingers to the stem and carefully measured an infinitesimal amount of energy. I gently released my power into the stem, asking the plant if it wished to link. My fingertips were rewarded with a familiar excited pulse, as if I was holding a hummingbird. Smiling at the flurry of acceptance I received from the plant, I merged my magic with its life force and delicately transmitted more power. My smile grew in tandem with the white, trumpet shaped flowers as the moonflower's lemony fragrance drifted through the air.

I quickly repeated the same actions with the rest of the vegetation, and within minutes, we were buried in lush greenery.

Adrian was enraptured as he watched the foliage grow all around us. I tracked his gaze, and his reaction to the life surrounding him reflected genuine pleasure. It was mesmerizing to see his joy, and I couldn't look away from his eyes. They were wide with fascination and awe; it was as if he was discovering magic for the first time.

He chuckled as a rapidly growing vine rose taller than him. He couldn't stop smiling and his eyes grew misty. I had never seen him so captivated.

He turned to me, still beaming. He started to thank me but caught himself.

I smiled, pleased to have made his day. "I'll tell you what, you can thank me by giving me a key to this rooftop. After all, I can keep everything thriving." Secretly, I was hoping he would not turn me down because the rooftop was amazing. Standing among the plants, I could feel my magic and body rejuvenate. It was the best I had felt in a very long time.

Adrian threw his hands up like he was surrendering. "And here I thought I was the one that was going to be showing you something amazing."

"You did," I said as his eyes shone in the moonlight. "But there's always room for improvement. It took the two of us together to bring out the best in these plants—your vision and my magic."

Adrian stared at me intensely, as if he could see directly into my soul. "Indeed," he whispered.

We stood there for some time, soaking in the moonlight and each other.

Intoxicating. That was the only way to explain it. Nothing else mattered. We couldn't see the buildings of Adrian's domain as the forest grew around us. The rest of the world disappeared. None of our current problems mattered, and neither did the past complications.

Adrian and I—a vampire and a fae—were in our own world, surrounded by teeming life.

CHAPTER SEVEN

The Catalyst

As I followed the familiar path home, Adrian's face lingered in my mind. Something profound had occurred on that rooftop. I knew I was walking a very precarious line. I had always been physically attracted to Adrian Sutton. It was impossible not to be. He was roguishly elegant with his gorgeous face, thick locks, soulful eyes, and lean-muscled body.

But physical allure was only that. Adrian was handsome, no doubt, but my attraction to his appearance was not the cause of my concern. Instead, I was reflecting on the mutual fondness we had for each other. The way we looked at each other. The warring feelings of trepidation and elation whenever I was near the undead monarch addled me.

My introspection took me to a horrible occurrence that happened two years prior, when a rogue vampire had attacked a little boy and Adrian rushed the child to me. That day forever changed us. Luckily, I was able to save the child's life as he lay in Adrian's blood-soaked arms. It wasn't until it was over, after I'd healed the boy's wounds and waited for him to take a few solid breaths, that I deigned to look into the eyes of the king of all vampires.

What I saw...there are no words. I'm not sure what happened to Adrian at that moment, but when our gazes met, I beheld utter astonishment mixed with jubilation. The unmitigated intensity of his emotion made it feel as though we were suspended in time, connected in some undefinable manner. Just as I started to ask him what was occurring, the boy's mother ran into the room, screaming. My gaze diverted from Adrian's for the briefest of moments, and when I found his eyes again, they were filled with a devastating anguish. The chaos of the situation at hand took precedence and Adrian handed the boy to his mother, offered me a beleaguered half-smile and nod, and left the room.

We never discussed it again, but that experience irrevocably changed our relationship. Something extremely intimate had occurred between us, but I wasn't sure what, exactly. I only knew that since that day, I'd felt a pull toward Adrian that I had not before, and I was not the only one who was affected. Adrian's interactions with me became considerably more personal. I went from being the healer down the hall to someone he regularly associated with. The differences were subtle, at first.

He began to take daily walks around the compound, checking in on everyone. He'd come by my small office and casually ask about my day, sometimes even inquiring about Dustin.

Adrian's visits were typically after lunch, and I often had tea steeping in my mug. Being British, he took particular interest in my tea habits and started inquiring as to my flavor preferences. One day, he made a point of showing me the proper way to make English afternoon tea, complete with loose leaf tea, warmed milk, sugar, and a tea cosy. I remembered thinking it was odd that Adrian Sutton, the vampire king, was in my office, and insisted on laboring over a cup of tea, but I also remembered that it made me smile.

He would nonchalantly chat with me, occasionally joking while emitting his alluring charm. I discussed his visits with Dustin and the Guardians, and everyone agreed that the increased interactions with Adrian were positive. They offered me opportunities to learn more about him and the inner workings of the seethe. I came to the same conclusion; however, there was a tiny part of me—a personal part that I tried desperately to ignore—who enjoyed his attention.

As the days and months passed, Adrian began to trust me more and more. He'd bounce ideas and thoughts off me, and eventually shared his concerns and fears as well. We developed a working companion-ship, and neither of us ever crossed a professional line.

I found myself wanting to know more about him on a personal level. There had been moments at home with Dustin when my errant thoughts turned to Adrian. Did he sit alone during his off hours and watch television? Did he sleep at night or was he out roaming the city streets? Was he lonely? Did he ever think of me?

Ugh! Goddess help me. What was I doing? I could *not* have feelings for Adrian Sutton. He was my assignment. He was a vampire. Every-one in my life would advise me that acting upon any type of interest in the vampire monarch would be a monumental mistake. I knew this. I agreed with it. But...the heart wants what it wants. As disturbing as it was, I was more and more emotionally drawn to Adrian during each moment we shared.

Dustin was home, unfortunately. I would have loved to have more time to process my thoughts. I should have just kept walking, but I was already late, and Dustin had not accompanied me home, as he usually did.

When he heard me come in, my supposed husband's eyes lifted from what he was reading. He looked pleased to have me home. Still, no matter how enthusiastic he was, I had trouble reciprocating.

Even though our marriage was only for show, I knew Dustin was in love with me. I could see it in his eyes every time he looked at me.

Our arrangement was straightforward, but I knew it hurt him, and I didn't want that. I cared deeply for Dustin as my coworker and friend, but there was no romantic love there, not on my part, anyway.

"Welcome home, Moira," he said. He walked over and leaned in for a kiss. His lips brushed my cheek, and I managed a smile, but that was all I could do. As usual, he looked disappointed when he backed away.

"Where were you? I came to your office to walk you home, and your things were there, but you were nowhere to be found. Finally, I caught your scent heading for the stairwell. Yours and Adrian's." His top lip curled back as he looked at me expectantly. *Crap.*

Being a cheetah shifter, he had a short fuse.

"Dustin, I'm sorry if I worried you. Can we discuss this later? I'm so tired. I just want to take a bath and lie down for a little while. It was an exhausting day."

I moved past him to head to the bedroom, but he turned to follow, unwilling to end the conversation. "We will have to call my parents soon. It's been a while since we spoke with them," he said curtly.

I had never spoken to Dustin's parents; they weren't alive, but most people didn't know that. The terminology was a code we'd established to discuss our employers because the apartment we lived in was owned by the seethe. It was how Adrian maintained a close watch on his employees and always knew where they were, even during off-hours. Dustin and I regularly checked the apartment for listening devices, but consistently preferred coded speech, regardless. Other people wouldn't understand the reference to Dustin's parents, but I knew what his words meant—the Guardians wanted an update about the vampires.

Being undercover was not too difficult, but we'd infiltrated Adrian's seethe five years ago, and the edges were beginning to fray. In some ways, I enjoyed playing a part and slipping into another life. I could be the quiet, dutiful wife; I could put on the mask of Mrs. Collins and pretend my marriage to my husband meant the world to me.

The longer we remained in our sham of a marriage, though, the harder it became. Pretending every hour of every day chipped away at my brain. Sometimes, I would forget that we were even married or that I couldn't talk about my actual work. I had to be the fae that helped heal vampires, that was all.

But reality and truth kept seeping in.

I took a breath and collected my thoughts, finding the fragile pieces of Mrs. Collins that were falling apart in my brain. I needed to center myself and remember who I was trying to be. No matter what I wanted or how it made me feel, what happened on that roof was not in line with what I should have been doing. Moira Collins, the wife of Dustin Collins and an unassuming fae healer, would never have made those plants flourish. It wasn't right, and it was a risk that I could not afford to take.

I turned back to my husband. "Then we should talk to them, don't you think?"

It was frustrating to have to give our superiors updates. It was dangerous and taking that kind of chance made it more challenging to be an undercover spy. Our assignment was to get close to Adrian Sutton and his inner circle, observe them, and report on their underhanded dealings and operations.

Dustin had no problem doing any of that, and I didn't either, at least not until an hour before. But something had changed on that rooftop with Adrian. Guilt suddenly welled in my gut at the thought of telling his enemies about his business. Unsuccessfully, I tried to push the feeling away.

My happiness on the rooftop didn't matter—it could never matter. There was too much work to be done.

CHAPTER EIGHT

A King's Duty

I t took a lot to impress Adrian, but Moira continued to surprise him. It wasn't just the power she had, it was that she had taken the time to give him a few minutes of reprieve and joy when most of his days were spent appeasing his fellow vampires.

For the first time in a long time, his responsibilities did not consume his thoughts. Instead, he saw an endless forest of green and a beautiful fae standing amid it all, smiling at him. He loved how the moonlight shined on her red hair, highlighting its vibrant colors.

"My king."

Adrian was ripped from his daydream of that beautiful, secret place where only he and Moira existed. When he resurfaced, he found Royce staring at him. His adviser's eternally middle-aged face was much less pleasing to behold than Moira's.

He was in the middle of a conversation with his adviser; mostly, it was just Royce droning on about why it was necessary to maintain friendships in the face of adversity. He disagreed with Adrian's decision to borrow blood from Bastien Champagne. Those willful eyes stared at him dubiously. "Are you listening, sire?"

"Yes, yes," Adrian lied, waving a dismissive hand at Royce. "Bastien needs that blood to keep his business flourishing, and the more successful his restaurants are, the more information he can glean from his patrons. I know. But it's not like we cleaned him out of all the blood. He had plenty to let us borrow. Besides, I'm his king. He should have no problem loaning us some of his supply."

"We need his spy network more than ever if we hope to find out who attacked us. And it may only be a small amount of blood in the grand scheme of things now, but what happens when this unseen enemy takes out more of our trucks? What happens when they make the transportation of goods impossible?"

"We won't let that happen." He meant that. Adrian didn't like being portrayed as a fool. The disruption of his blood supply was merely a fluke; that was all. Regardless, he wasn't going to allow another attack. "We will have some of our best men guarding those trucks. I will even go myself."

"Out of the question," Royce snapped. "Taking that kind of risk when you know there are enemies—"

Adrian's gaze whipped to Royce. Friendship and loyalty aside, the king of the vampires did not concede to anyone. "I will always have enemies. And in case you have forgotten, my friend, I don't take orders from anyone. You can disagree with me, but I am going to go out there and protect my blood. Understand?"

Royce backed down as he always did when Adrian stood up to him. He was opinionated and he occasionally forgot his place, but he was always quick to get back in line.

Royce cleared his throat, flicked his eyes at Adrian, and then back down again. "There is another reason for my concern, sire. I spoke with the men who were attacked last night."

Royce had his king's full attention. "And?" inquired Adrian.

"And..." began Royce, pausing to squeeze his upper lip with his bottom teeth, "the soldiers...our men...it seems the reports from Kellan and Moira Collins were accurate; they nearly met their true death. One was killed; the other seven were some of our strongest vampires."

Royce's level of discomfort was evident and disturbing to Adrian. Royce was typically unflappable, so the fact that the condition of the soldiers shook him was disturbing. "Did they say who attacked them?"

"That's just it. The men couldn't see anything. Each rig held two men in the cab and two in the trailer, guarding the blood. The next thing they knew, the lead rig ran over something that popped the tires. He slowed to a stop, and the rig behind him did the same. They followed their training protocol. The cab soldiers got out to investigate while the others remained in the rear of the trucks." Royce ran his fingers through his gray hair.

"The four men from the truck cabs covered each other, but an unseen source launched smoke bombs laced with poison at the group. It rendered our soldiers numb and caused them to hallucinate, so it was probably aconite. They don't remember anything coherent after the poison did its job. The men in the cargo area of the trucks said they heard the explosions but remained in place, guarding the blood." Royce nodded, silently approving the actions of the men.

He continued, "Someone or something jumped on top of the trucks, ripped a hole in the roofs, and dropped more of those poisoned bombs in. The men managed to open the rear doors and escape, but they were attacked. They don't remember much at all." Royce's worried eyes met Adrian's.

"Someone knew their exact routes and our emergency protocols," Adrian said as he turned to stare at the wall to his right. "But why weren't they killed? Whoever did this was able to finish them off, yet they didn't. Why?" he asked, looking at Royce.

His adviser stood, staring back at his king. "Who knows? Maybe they ran out of time? Maybe they thought they would die from their injuries?"

"Or maybe they wanted to send a message...to me," Adrian posited.

Royce said nothing; he simply watched Adrian. "Maybe they wanted me to know that they held the power of life and death over my people. Think about it. If all our men had been killed, they would be ash now, with no bodies to see, no wounds to heal. We would have never known how much damage they took. This way, someone very clearly demonstrated their power and used the bodies of our soldiers to make a point. It is a play for dominance. Someone out there is perpetrating a perilous game, which I intend to win. Now, more than ever, I know for certain that I need to be the one on those streets tonight. I need to end this."

Royce bowed his head and said, "As you wish, my king." Then, he shuffled into the hall, casting one last look over his shoulder before turning the corner.

Watching his adviser walk away, Adrian took a deep breath and wrestled with his frustration. Royce's information worried him. There was a traitor in his camp. He had potentially offended Bastien by demanding some of his blood supply. Who was planning this coup against him? Was it more than one ringmaster? How long had this been in motion? What was coming next? He was surrounded by dozens of people who could betray him at any moment. He had questions, but no answers.

Despite his concern for the seethe, his thoughts turned to the beautiful redheaded fae. He was responsible for the safety of his people, and he knew it was his duty to focus on the task at hand. Moira was a distraction, and he vowed to put her out of his head.

It wasn't fair, but his seethe had to come first, at least for now.

CHAPTER NINE

Protect the Blood

Kellan Fallon fidgeted in his seat, toying with the hem of his shirt as he looked around the room, no doubt still reeling from the previous night's attacks. He knew that the transportation of the blood was his responsibility. While they'd never had a prior problem with them, his duty was to ensure that the red rigs were protected, and the blood safely reached its destination. It was his failure.

Adrian was already missing the more carefree version of Kellan. He was usually fun to be around and lived his immortal life to the fullest. Now, he was walking on eggshells, terrified to make another mistake.

Kellan unfolded a city map and spread it on the table so Adrian could see. He ran his finger along roads to show him the red rigs' routes. Adrian was already aware of these, but he didn't interrupt. After pointing out the paths, Kellan began specifying locations.

"We have some of our people here and here." Then, using a thick red marker, he circled all the places where vampires were going to be stationed to provide extra security for the trucks. "That should be enuf' to fight off any bastards that decide to give us trouble." Still looking down at the map, Kellan nodded, almost as if he was reassuring himself.

"If it's not, I will be there, too."

Kellan looked stunned to hear that. "What d'ya mean that—"

"I like to protect my investments, especially when they are under attack."

Relief swept over Kellan, and his signature Cheshire grin finally returned to his face. "Well then, I'm guess'n we've got nothin' to worry about, eh?" he said, his Irish brogue in full swing.

That was flattering, but Adrian didn't necessarily agree. They still didn't know what they were battling. Hopefully, they would learn soon enough.

As Adrian prepared to patrol that night, he was greeted by Felicia Lorne, the last person he thought he'd encounter.

"I didn't expect to see you around. I figured you would be thousands of miles away by now. I know you are not the biggest fan of Hell's Kitchen."

Felicia gave him a half-hearted smile. "It's not that I am not a fan of it. The fact is, there are many places in the world that offer so much more."

"I'm surprised you aren't in one of those places, then."

"I delayed my departure because I wanted to ensure that I was on hand in case you needed more assistance."

"You think you would be the deciding factor?"

Felicia crossed her arms over her voluptuous chest. "I think I know my worth, yes. I'm sure you have everything under control. I am curious how you intend to stop these saboteurs."

Adrian slipped his hands into the pockets of his black slacks and assumed a casual slouch. He did not want to appear worried in front of Felicia. "We find out who they are, what they want, and what kind of a threat they pose. Then, we eliminate the threat."

Eyebrows raised, Felicia retorted, "That sounds simple enough, but only if the ones doing this are pushovers. If it is the Usurpers or the Guardians, you might have a genuine problem. They won't go down easily. You might need reinforcements."

"I will keep you in mind," Adrian conceded. "But I can't promise we will see any real combat during this."

"I hope we do," Felicia said as her gaze drifted from Adrian's, lost in thought. "I would love to let out some pent-up energy and getting our hands on someone would be a good way of gathering more information."

Felicia didn't like to get her hands dirty, but when she did, it always spelled trouble for her adversaries. She usually maintained a tight grip on her emotions and preferred to portray a more reserved demeanor. But simmering beneath the surface was a woman capable of extreme acts of violence. She had no qualms about her brutality; that was part of what made her extremely dangerous, but it also made her an excellent ally.

Adrian studied her and cocked his head, asking, "How has it been in the rest of the world?"

Felicia looked taken aback by the question; she seemed surprised that he would even ask. She blinked and shrugged. "Same as always. Most of our kind still cower in the dark with little assistance. They are purely nocturnal predators, and even that can be dangerous. It's not like it is here in Hell's Kitchen. They don't have the same support, and there are few safe havens." She eyed Adrian, measuring his response.

It was evident from her tone that she held some resentment about that. Adrian knew he focused too much on what was nearby and didn't give enough thought to his people out in the further reaches of the world. They were cut off from places like Hell's Kitchen, where they weren't treated like bloodsucking parasites. There was always more that he could do for them, but he was spread thin. He relied on his Council members and the network he'd created to oversee his global outreach. However, it was clear there were holes in the organization that needed to be filled.

"What are you suggesting I do?" He asked the question even though he already knew her answer. Felicia was predictable, and they'd had this conversation before.

"You could unshackle yourself from this place and look outward."

There it was. Felicia had never been a fan of Hell's Kitchen and constantly talked about the benefits of leaving. His opinion on the matter hadn't swayed over the years.

"And you would have me do what, exactly? Remind me; it's been a while since I last had to shoot this idea down. Do you think I should start finding new lands for us? Should I expand into other territories? That would be easy enough, right? Oh wait, that would be trespassing at best, and an act of war at worst. We've had this tired discussion, and the conversation ended long ago."

Felicia held up a finger, shaking it in protest as she retorted, "No, you ended the conversation before we had a chance to talk it through."

"That's because no amount of persuasion was going to convince me to become a conqueror!" Adrian snapped.

"Then you are fine with this? You're content knowing our people are growing more and more stagnant with every decade. You may not see it here, but the vampires beyond the borders of Hell's Kitchen are starving."

"Felicia! Starving? Really? I hardly think being relegated to eating bagged blood and feeding only at night in certain regions is starving. I'd thank you to stop exaggerating in such a manner. You and I both know this is not an argument about hunger. You wish for us to be superior to other creatures, which is unsustainable. One way or another, the seethe would be wiped out by those who disagree."

Adrian shook his head in disgust as he held up a hand and counted off one finger at a time as he spoke. "We have the Usurpers on one side, the Guardians on the other, then the humans, shifters, and other species who live here. We all need to coexist on this planet. If the vampires make a major move against any of those factions, all-out war will ensue."

Eyes narrowing, Adrian continued, "If your words are true and our people are starving, then perhaps I need to reevaluate my choice of Council members. After all, I've set up blood drives worldwide, and you, my Council members, are responsible for your respective regions. So, if I supply the blood to each region and our people are starving, then whose fault is that?" Adrian spread his hands and glared at Felicia. "I can promise you that no one in my region is starving. So, tell them to come to us, and I will personally ensure they are given the best meals they have ever had."

Mouth dropping open, Felicia raged, "That's not the point! Are you really going to stay here and walk these same tired streets for eternity? You have all the time in the world and you should use it to do something important! To help vampires not just survive, but flourish! Thrive!"

"Ah yes, I should be a king and an emperor, too. Let's march our forces into troll territory or overthrow the elves. Let's sacrifice countless of our kind so we can take land we don't need and prove that we are the most dominant species on the planet. What could possibly go wrong?" Adrian paced back and forth in front of Felicia. He stopped at each turn to glare in her direction.

Felicia scowled and scoffed, as she'd done the first five times she pitched her imperial idea. It sounded unappealing to him, just as it had in those initial arguments. His stance hadn't changed, and neither had hers. She could complain all she wanted, but it was his kingdom. Starting a war was not high on his priority list. While the vampires were powerful, they didn't have the strength or numbers to overcome the rest of the world. They were immortal, but they were not invincible.

If only Felicia could see his perspective, but she didn't even try to.

"I think it's time you get back out there," Adrian said firmly, making his command clear. "I'm sure you have much work to do in other countries. But, as you can see, we are doing perfectly fine here."

Adrian didn't need Felicia sticking around the compound to instigate age-old debates. There were more pressing things to worry about, but she didn't seem nearly as interested in those issues. Despite their long history, Adrian could only take so much of her. The briefer the visit, the better.

Felicia rolled her eyes, and Adrian, using vamp speed, flashed across the room to stand in front of her. His menacing stare bored into her, a direct challenge to her blatant disrespect. Felicia held his gaze for a micro-second, lowered her eyes, stepped back two paces, and bowed. No matter how often she spoke out, she knew there were lines she should not cross. Still, she tried to have the last passive-aggressive word. "I hope Hell's Kitchen continues to thrive."

Adrian fired right back. "Oh, I can assure you, it will. Safe travels, Felicia."

Adrian didn't need Felicia's help stopping the perpetrators. He was more than capable of dealing with them on his own. The vampire king had not survived the past six hundred years by being weak, but Adrian thought his subjects needed a reminder.

Although he would never admit it, Felicia's words stung. She accused him of sitting in a glass tower while his people suffered. In truth, Adrian had not left the safety and comfort of Hell's Kitchen in a very long time.

Knowing what he had to do, Adrian returned to his rooftop retreat, where the plants he and Moira had cultivated offered a welcome reprieve to the monochromatic colors of the surrounding buildings. He ran his hand through the vegetation as he walked to the edge of the building.

Adrian sighed as he leaned his elbows on the brick ledge and peered at his kingdom. As much as people looked down on the neighborhood, he appreciated its rough-hewn qualities. Adrian toiled and struggled for years to turn Hell's Kitchen into a vampire sanctuary that supported his community's growth—but that safety had now been tarnished.

Someone dared to interfere with his business, burn his trucks, and attack his soldiers. It was unacceptable, and his enemies would answer for their actions. He would ensure they never harmed him, his people, or his operations again.

A vampire was at their most potent when night first fell. Closing his eyes and inhaling deeply, he allowed the darkness to envelop him and seep into his body. It was euphoric.

He glanced at the plants on the roof. Their beauty was still radiant even in the dark, thanks to the infusion of Moira's magic. But he hadn't come up to the roof to admire them. Instead, the vantage point held another fundamental purpose.

Flight was a rare power that only the oldest of vampires acquired. They had spent so long separated from their mortality, from the graves they would never see, that the earth untethered them from its gravitational grip. It had taken Adrian more than a couple of centuries to tap into the ability.

Adrian let himself fall forward and plummeted from the rooftop. The night sky took hold of him and pulled him upward as he ascended through the air. Flying above Hell's Kitchen, the shadows became his wings. His body was weightless as he soared across the starry sky.

Adrian's domain was peaceful enough for the time being, but he kept moving toward the truck routes. If anything were to happen, he would have a good view of what was going on from the air. It was also the perfect place to ambush the attackers and make them regret their challenge.

Flying was a quiet thing. That high up, Adrian could barely hear the world below; the only sounds that reached him were car horns, alarms, and sirens. Everything was far beneath him, and Hell's Kitchen seemed like an ant farm.

The cool breeze helped to clear his head of errant thoughts. Tonight's mission wasn't just about intercepting an attack on his trucks or ending those responsible. He also planned to discover how they knew about the routes, as the trucks were unmarked and regularly changed their paths, days, and travel times.

He kept track of the streets, knowing the exact course his red rigs would take. He dipped lower to better understand the specifics of the roads below. When he found one of the red rigs moving toward its destination, he flew above it, keeping pace and eyeing the others nearby.

The blood transportation vehicles maintained reasonable proximity to one another, but it was also a point of vulnerability that Adrian intended to correct once he found the attackers. Tonight, he wanted the route to follow the intended schedule. With extra security below and Adrian above, his trucks and the blood would be safe.

Just as he finished thinking about their advantage, he heard the unmistakable sound of tires popping. Adrian's fury crashed through him as the truck veered onto the sidewalk and rammed into a building.

A group of shadows emerged from the darkness, running toward the crippled vehicle. Adrian hurtled toward the scene like a meteor when he saw the attackers. He landed between the truck and the ones planning to destroy it.

The group wore gas masks and carried firearms. A gun usually wasn't much of a threat to a vampire, but given enough bullets, they could cause significant damage—at least to vampires under two hundred years old. At Adrian's age, most bullets posed no more threat than a buzzing fly.

However, Adrian needed to find out what the weapons were designed to do. At first glance, they were more prominent than a typical automatic rifle. Though the weapons were styled like an AR-15, the barrel of each gun was broader, and the magazines held unknown ammunition.

Observing the men cautiously, Adrian said, "You should have moved on after your little stunt last night. Did you think I would allow that to happen again?"

The men didn't respond. Instead, they raised their weapons. Adrian stared down a dozen gun barrels. It would have intimidated most people—but the vampire king was not most people.

Adrian contemplated tearing off their masks and seeing the fools beneath. He needed to know who was behind the blatant attack on his community, and he planned to punish them severely.

The door to the truck opened, and Kellan Fallon jumped out. He didn't notice the gunmen as he swore at the popped tires. When he turned to see what was happening, he laughed.

"I decided to protect the trucks personally this time, my king," Kellan said, joining Adrian. "If'n ya' want sumthin' done right, ya' have to do it yourself, aye?"

"That's right," Adrian said. "Which is why you should make sure the other trucks haven't been hit as well. I will handle things here."

Kellan looked a little disappointed. He probably wanted to fight alongside his king and prove his worth to make up for the previous night's mistakes. Adrian, however, did not like to share his prey. They had already marked themselves for death when they pointed their guns at him.

Kellan complied and disappeared into the darkness, leaving Adrian alone with the enemy. From their size alone, they didn't look like giants or trolls. Of course, finding any valuable identifiers would be challenging with the masks, but a vampire's senses trumped facial coverings.

Adrian sniffed in their direction. They had a familiar scent; the musty, ever-dying stench of mortals permeated most of the world.

"Humans." Adrian shook his head.

Humans offered him no challenge, and he initially thought he had nothing to worry about. Then, all at once, the men fired.

Instinctually, Adrian turned his body to the side so the projectiles would not lodge in his heart. As the barrage pelted him, he discovered they were not bullets. Instead, the magazines were filled with wooden spikes, and they'd been dipped in poison—probably aconite, like the smoke bombs.

As the skewers entered his body, Adrian started to panic. Hundreds of the tiny missiles flew through the air, and only one needed to pierce his heart to bring him true death. To make matters worse, the numbing agent in the aconite slowed his movements, and the hallucinations began.

Usually, Adrian enjoyed a challenge. The panic on his opponent's face when they realized what they were up against always brought him joy, but this time was different. For the first time in his life, the humans were the ones smiling. Ironically, the hubris of the men enraged Adrian and gave him the wherewithal to call upon his century's old strength and speed.

He flashed to the nearest human, snapping his neck, and turning him to use as a human shield. The other men fired, pelting the human meat sack with wooden stakes. Adrian ripped into the man's neck, greedily swallowing his blood before the aconite had time to taint it. As he did so, he felt the poison dissipate in his system. Then, still clutching his limp shield, he flashed to another attacker.

Adrian threw the man he carried at his new target, and as his second victim ducked, the vampire king struck. He drank his new prey dry, shielding his body as he did so.

The hot, crimson blood surged through Adrian like liquid electricity. It provided instant healing and renewed his strength. As the stakes were forced from his flesh, Sir Adrian Sutton offered his enemies a wicked, blood-stained grin.

The ten remaining men still wore their masks, but Adrian did not miss the sag of their shoulders and their nervous glances as they began to back away.

Their heartbeats accelerated, pounding away inside their chests. The sound became a grisly chorus, and Adrian reveled in their fear.

"What is the matter? I thought you wanted to destroy the truck." He nodded toward the trailer. "Don't tell me you plan to bugger off now? The fun has just begun."

Three of the humans mustered up the courage to draw wooden stakes from the insides of their coats, perhaps thinking they would help if Adrian appeared near them. He had made it clear that they could no longer shoot him.

"I like when people make it interesting. Please try to live long enough for me to enjoy myself."

Without another word, he dropped the body and pounced on his prey. His recent blood intake had returned him to full strength, and his speed ensured he was nothing more than a dark blur in their eyes, at least while he was moving. The last thing they would see when he slowed down was his fangs.

The three with the stakes died first. Adrian didn't need to take any risks. He broke their necks one by one with a simple flick of his wrist. Their weapons clattered to the pavement as they fell.

The others desperately fired their guns, but they didn't have a chance. Now that Adrian understood the weapons, he could easily dodge their assault.

Adrian enjoyed the next few minutes as he lost himself in the blood-lust. He eradicated the humans like the vermin they were, ravaging their throats and tearing their hearts from their chests. Fresh blood was unmatched.

Adrian didn't hear the screams until there was only one man left. The sole survivor tried to crawl away, but the vampire king wouldn't let him go—at least not yet. The man was sobbing and gasping for air. He was clearly untrained.

Adrian tucked his hands in his pockets and followed, quickly catching up to the escaping man. Then, he grabbed the weakling by the back of his jacket and suspended him in mid-air, like a cat being held up by the scruff of his neck.

The terrified human was a pathetic sight. But unsurprisingly, he didn't try to break free or defend himself; the man knew his mortal life would end much sooner if he fought.

"Do you know who I am?" Adrian asked.

The human didn't answer. Tears poured down his cheeks, and his teeth chattered with nerves. He kept his eyes closed, not daring to open them as he waited for his inevitable death.

Adrian didn't like being ignored, no matter the reason. "Look at me!"

Slowly, the man's eyes widened, and he peeked through his eyelids. Then, through his shivering and crying, he begged, "Don't! Please don't! Please!"

Adrian burst out laughing, keeping the man suspended in the air. "Give me one good reason why I shouldn't."

"I have a family!"

"So do I," Adrian said with a shrug. "And you and your friends here want to hurt them. I'm sure you can see why that might make me upset. Now answer my question, do you know who I am?" The man bit his tear-soaked lip and shook his head. "Adrian Sutton. The king of the vampires. Please tell me you have at least heard of me."

The human shook his head once again.

Adrian wasn't surprised. The knobhead was most likely hired muscle. Also, he had made a point to keep the vampire seethe hidden from humans. Nevertheless, Adrian intended to give himself a proper introduction.

Adrian let the shadows envelop him again, and the night sky slowly raised him and his unwitting passenger off the street, lifting them above the nearby buildings. He hovered there with the screaming man flailing in his grasp.

The ascent hadn't helped his victim's panic or his furiously beating heart, which was ready to burst. "Bloody hell." Adrian curled his lip in disgust as the scent of urine reached his sensitive nose.

"Please! You have to put me down! Please!"

"Do you know what that is?"

Adrian allowed the horrified man to dangle, giving him a good view of the city beneath them.

"That is Hell's Kitchen, the epicenter of my dominion. I built it from the ground up. Everything you see down there belongs to me. My people and our livestock. That is the place you have tried to damage. So, you can see why I can't let that slide."

"I didn't know! I didn't—I swear!"

Adrian didn't care about the man's plea, only about the information he sought.

"Who put you up to this? Who told you to attack my trucks?"

"I...I don't know!" The man looked like he was about to pass out. He was barely able to formulate coherent thoughts, let alone speak them aloud, but Adrian kept pushing.

"What do you mean you don't know!?"

"I don't remember! I don't!"

Adrian loosened his grip and let the man think he was about to fall, prompting a new wave of tears. It served as a reminder of what was at stake.

"What do you remember, then?"

The man shut his eyes like he was trying to force the memories out of his skull. He stuttered and gasped, but he finally choked out a reply. "I...I know there was a person...yes...they came, and they hired us. They said...they said it was going to be easy money! A quick series of jobs! That was what they said!"

"Does this feel like easy money?" Adrian growled, loosening his hold a bit more.

"I'm sorry! I'm so, so sorry! Please let me down! Please!"

"I will once you tell me who paid you to interfere in my business."

The human's mind was nearly broken. He was a mess of terror, tears, piss, and sweat.

"I can't. I don't know why, but I can't remember...their face is...I don't know what their face looks like. I just remember looking into their eyes. They said something about forgetting them...I guess they were right."

Of course. The answer became apparent to Adrian. The person paying them to target the trucks had compelled them to do so. Afterward, they must have stripped their identity from the men's memories. Compulsion was an ability almost exclusive to vampires; they could reach into the minds of mortals and hypnotically persuade them to do whatever they wanted. It wasn't an easy power to control, which indicated experience.

The thought of his own people turning against him, conspiring to damage him and his operations, hurt more than anything. This confirmed it with absolute certainty. There was a traitor in his midst.

"Please...I've told you everything I know...can you please, for the love of God, let me go?"

"I have never been a fan of God," Adrian said. "Thank you for your cooperation."

Adrian let go of the man and watched him plummet through the air, screaming the entire way down to his death.

The king of vampires didn't regret the night's carnage. The humans were their source of sustenance and nothing more, and the casualties would be quickly brushed aside. They weren't what was important—the vampire who puppeteered them was the one who really mattered.

As he descended to the street below, Adrian contemplated his situation. He had done nothing but try to serve his people as best as possible, and none of his actions warranted this betrayal.

He would find his Judas.

CHAPTER TEN

Enemies are Circling

T he rest of the night was uneventful. No other trucks were attacked, but Adrian knew the real enemy still posed a threat.

When Adrian returned to the compound, covered in human blood,
he briefed his adviser on what occurred. Royce's face conveyed warring
expressions of longing and disgust as he regarded the red splatter on
Adrian's pristine white shirt. Part of him no doubt craved the life-giv-
ing liquid, while the other part despised the mess.

Royce was good at appearing insouciant by the news, but his silence
was deafening. He was in deep thought, strategically working the
puzzle in his mind.

"There is a traitor in our midst, then," he said, with determination
in his steely eyes. "I will drain the Council dry so I can dive into their
minds; the few drops I normally sample may not have been enough to
expose their deception. Then, if I determine they are innocent, I will
go through every vampire we have ever turned until we find the truth.
There will be no exceptions."

Royce always went to the furthest extremes when challenged. Unfortunately, he didn't think about the repercussions of his behavior. The actions he suggested would cause community-wide panic and resentment among the vampires. Sure, it might reveal the traitor, but it would just as likely turn their own people against them.

"Let's hold off on forming an inquisition," Adrian said. "We'll find another way."

Royce scowled at Adrian and propped his hands on his hips.

Adrian removed his destroyed shirt and washed his face. His adviser grew more relaxed as the blood ran down the drain.

"What would you suggest, my king?" Royce asked.

"Isn't that what you are here for? To offer me suggestions and nudge me in the right direction."

Royce gave a humorless laugh. "I have tried to do just that, but you often refuse to be nudged."

"I guess that's fair."

Their conversation was interrupted by a brief knock on the ajar office door as it slowly pushed open. Moira stood at the threshold, looking concerned. She was out of breath like she had rushed to find them.

She brushed some of her red hair away from her face.

"Is everyone okay? Kellan sent me here and said I might need to do some mending."

"That Irishman always underestimates me." Adrian snickered, pushing his arms into the sleeves of a clean, white shirt. He couldn't help but notice Moira glancing at his chest as he slipped the button-up over his shoulders. "But no, we are more than fine. The saboteurs could've used some fae magic, but it's too late for them."

"Oh…" Moira seemed a little lost. "Okay, well, let me know if you need me. I'll be downstairs."

She turned to leave, but Adrian had other plans.

"Moira, wait."

She turned, looking at him expectantly.

"Would you like to go out to dinner tonight? A working dinner, of course. It's on me."

Moira blinked. She opened her mouth to speak but then shut it again. She glanced uncomfortably at Royce and then back to Adrian. "You and me?"

Adrian shrugged. "Just us. Need to bounce some ideas off you."

"I don't know that Dustin would be okay with it. He might have plans for us for tonight—"

"He won't," Adrian interrupted matter-of-factly. "I have a job that requires his services this evening, so your schedule is clear."

Moira stared at him for a long moment; she had no reason not to share a meal with him now. But he could see that it wasn't all anxiousness and concern. There was a flash of excitement on her face, too.

"Um...okay. Sure, why not?"

"Brilliant. I'll pick you up at your apartment after the sun goes down."

Moira stepped away with a furrowed brow.

Royce stood by the wall, having observed the whole exchange with his usual quiet contemplation. He was a thoughtful man who only spoke when he felt strongly about something. When those gray eyes fell upon Adrian, it was clear he had something to say.

"Are you sure that is wise?"

Adrian played dumb. He did not want to have this conversation. "Is what wise?"

Royce's face twitched before his expression hardened. He took one step forward, casting an air of cryptic uncertainty into the room. "I wonder if it is wise to fraternize with her."

Adrian shrugged. "You are the wise one here, my friend. Not me."

"In a time like this, when our enemies are circling and trying to starve us...you're taking an unnecessary risk consorting with a fae."

"Consorting?" Adrian's anger ignited and Royce took a small step back. "As if I'm consorting with the enemy? I am doing no such thing. Moira is one of us."

Royce's brow furrowed, and he shook his head. "She isn't."

"Bloody hell, Royce! She's not one of us, but she has been nothing but loyal. She is an asset to the seethe. The fact that she isn't like us makes her even less of a suspect. The prat I interrogated said he was hired by a vampire. And, as you pointed out, Moira is not a vampire!"

"That does not mean she can be trusted!" snapped Royce.

"Maybe not completely, but it does make her much less of a suspect than every other person in this building."

Royce let out a sardonic laugh. He was irate, but when Royce got angry, he became reticent and spoke with a soft, seething tone. "What a foolish thing to say. You have known me and many others in this building for hundreds of years, and you trust us less than an outsider with whom you have barely spent any real time."

That was the thing about vampires. They cared about the length of time spent together rather than the quality. Adrian knew he and Moira had spent real time together—those incredible minutes on the roof felt more valuable than the centuries he'd spent with some of his closest followers.

It would be impossible to explain any of that to someone like Royce, who simply didn't think that way. His adviser could only see the negatives that came with Moira's differences. The truth was Moira was not one of Adrian's subjects, and he was not her king. They were colleagues, and it was invigorating to enjoy the company of someone who was not a vampire.

"If you really doubt her intentions so much, go and feed on her memories," Adrian said sharply. "Oh, that's right. You can't. That's what this is about for you, Royce. You're nervous because she makes you feel powerless. You can't stand the fact that her blood tells you nothing."

Royce clenched his jaw and visibly struggled to keep his curled fists at his sides, but he fell silent. He knew there was at least some truth to what his king was saying.

"You don't have to trust her, my friend, but you do have to trust me. A fae is not our problem right now. We need to look inward to find the one that has broken their vow and turned on us."

Royce nodded, conceding the argument—for the time being, at least. "I'll get drops from everyone in the building and see if I discover anything. It's not guaranteed to work, but—"

"It's a start," Adrian said. "You get right on that. I have a dinner date to prepare for."

"Just do me one favor, my king."

Adrian turned back to his adviser.

"I think it would be wise to stay within Hell's Kitchen and the borders of our territory for the time being. While there may be a rat or two, most of our kind would still give their lives to protect you."

Adrian smiled. "Thank you for your wise counsel, my friend. I'll follow your guidance."

Royce maintained his stoic expression.

Chapter Eleven

Disrupted Plans

Had the king of the vampires just asked me on a date? I couldn't even begin to think how I would explain the situation to Dustin.

Though my mind was reeling with panic, I could not tamp down my giddiness. It felt like I was split down the middle, with one side screaming at me to immediately cease this interaction with Adrian, while the other wanted to run to him.

The time we'd spent on the rooftop, the conversations we'd had and the chemistry between us— I wanted more of that, which posed a considerable problem. I'd been working for Adrian for five years, and our emotional intimacy had grown during that time.

As much as I tried to remain neutral in his presence, I was undeniably attracted to him. The man oozed sex appeal, yet he was always a gentleman. Moreover, he never disrespected my marriage to Dustin; he kept us both gainfully employed and protected us as his own.

I struggled daily with intense guilt. I was guilty of being attracted to Adrian. I was guilty of spying on Adrian and reporting to the Guardians. I was guilty of faking a marriage with Dustin while spending time with another man. So, what was I going to do?

When I entered the apartment, Dustin was finishing a bug check, using a handheld detection device provided to us by the Guardians. He nodded to me, indicating that our vampire-owned dwelling was not being spied on, at least at the moment. His timing was serendipitous because I needed to speak freely.

There were a few boxes of take-out on the counter, and he grinned when he saw me. "Hey! Long day? I thought I would get us some dinner—"

"I actually have plans tonight."

His smile disappeared, but I needed to tell him. Being straightforward was usually the best way to communicate with Dustin. He didn't like riddles or lies.

"Plans tonight? Are the vampires having you do something for them?"

"Kind of." I internally cringed. Our marriage might not have been legitimate, but Dustin held a special place in my heart. He was my work partner and friend; I loved him like family and didn't want to hurt his feelings.

"Adrian Sutton invited me to dinner."

Dustin looked absolutely shell-shocked. "What?"

"He wants me to go out with him tonight," I said, hoping my serenity would rub off on Dustin. "He said he wanted to bounce some ideas off me."

"I'm sure that's all a vampire king wants," Dustin said, rolling his eyes. "This is a joke, right?"

"No," I said. "I'm sorry, but I don't really have a choice here. What am I supposed to do? Say no to the ruler of the vampires? We need an in with them, remember?"

"We have one! We already work for them!" Dustin snapped.

"Yes, but getting to know him personally could help us find things he wouldn't share otherwise." I could see I wasn't getting through to him. He peered dubiously at the take-out boxes, probably imagining how they would go to waste.

There was still one card I could play. "The Guardians would approve of this. Our assignment was to ingratiate ourselves as deeply as possible into the seethe. You can't get much deeper than a dinner date with the most important target."

Dustin visibly struggled with the plan, massaging the area between his eyes with his thumb and forefinger. "So, I'm just supposed to stay here alone while you're having dinner with a monster."

"I don't think Adrian poses a danger to me, to be honest."

Dustin crossed his arms over his chest and narrowed his eyes.

I continued before he could interrupt me, "It's been five years, and he could have easily attacked either one of us at the compound. So why would he suddenly take me off-site for some nefarious plot? It makes no sense. I'm pretty sure it would be much simpler for him to bleed me dry at work if that makes you feel better," I said coyly, trying to lighten the mood. "But I also don't think you will be here all night, either."

"What do you mean?" he asked, frowning.

Almost as if Adrian was listening in on our conversation, the phone rang. Dustin strode to the wall to answer it, and I could see from the frustration on his face that he was receiving orders. He curled his fingers around the handset like he wanted to strangle the life out of it.

Dustin spoke with vaguely camouflaged anger. "Uh-huh. Yeah. I got it. Yep. Will do."

Returning the phone to its cradle with more force than necessary, he turned to me, looking like he had just been played for a fool. "So, as it turns out, Sutton needs me to work a job tonight; it seems like we'll both be eating leftovers." Dustin only referred to Adrian by his last name when he was furious.

I shrugged. "Sorry. The struggles of being undercover."

Dustin frowned. "Right."

CHAPTER TWELVE

Dinner with a Vampire

The Belfry was not a restaurant that anyone other than vampires would usually deign to enter. The human residents of Hell's Kitchen were not welcome there—except perhaps as an addition to the menu. The restaurant was a feeding ground where vampires could have a dining experience explicitly catered to their unique dietary preferences.

There was a long line queued outside the expensive steakhouse. Adrian took my hand and led me straight to the front door, where two bouncers were ushering people in. They bowed their heads when they saw Adrian and opened the door for us.

I felt a little guilty when I glanced at the people we'd bypassed, but admittedly, it was nice to avoid the wait.

I leaned over to Adrian as we walked through the doors. "I guess there are some perks to wearing the crown."

Adrian smirked. "Just a couple."

The inside of The Belfry was somewhat different than I had imagined. It had a dark atmosphere, but beautiful, dim lights illuminated the entire dining room. The chandeliers appeared to have been plucked from different centuries, all beautiful and ornate in their own ways.

The ceiling was painted with a mural of a bat soaring through a starry skyscape. The whole place was breathtaking.

When we sat at a VIP table in the corner, Adrian looked up toward the balcony, which housed more seating. He raised his glass in a toast, and when I followed his gaze, I found a recognizable, well-dressed man leaning against the railing. I'd seen his face on several commercials, magazine articles, and billboards. It was the infamous Bastien Champagne.

There wasn't anyone in any part of New York City who didn't know Bastien's face. His restaurants were always busy, regardless of location. He had a way of appealing to everyone's appetites; it didn't matter what the demographic was.

Still, seeing him in his flagship restaurant in the heart of vampire territory was strange. It was even more bizarre when he looked in our direction, flashed his signature smile, and started to walk down the stairs toward our table.

Before he reached us, I turned to Adrian. "I didn't realize you were friends with Bastien Champagne."

"Oh, yes," Adrian confirmed. "Bastien and I go very far back. He is a busy man who doesn't frequent the compound very much. Well, ever, really. He is still a friend, though."

Bastien walked with the showmanship he was known for. It was the kind of confidence that radiated off the most influential of people. His charisma was infectious, and he charmed a room before he even said a word. The moment he got close, I couldn't help but pay attention to him. Of course, it didn't hurt that he was also very handsome.

"Well, look who decided to roll in for breakfast. His majesty himself!" Bastien gave a curt bow to his ruler but grinned from ear to ear the whole time. It was more of a mocking gesture than a respectful one, but Adrian didn't seem to mind. "I'm not used to seeing you so often. I do hope my delivery got to you in one piece."

"It did, thank you," Adrian said.

"Fantastic, fantastic," Bastien said. "Happy to do my part."

I didn't know what they were referring to, but I wasn't given much time to think about it. The restaurateur turned his attention—and his smile—in my direction. He held out an open palm expectantly. I gave him my hand, and he gently kissed the back of it.

"And who might you be, pretty lady?"

"Moira Collins."

"It's a pleasure to meet you, Miss Collins."

I stammered out a response without even thinking. "It's Mrs. Collins."

Bastien's smile turned into a look of confusion as he glanced at Adrian for an explanation. His grin soon returned, and he looked more impressed than ever. He clicked his tongue with mischief in his eyes. "My mistake. Is this your first time dining in one of my establishments, Mrs. Collins?"

"It is, yes," I said honestly.

Bastien clapped his hands as if excited by the news. "Perfect. And you are...pardon me asking...a fae, yes?"

Adrian narrowed his eyes at Bastien as I nodded, a little put off by the question. I was aware of several nosy vampires in the room who were directing far too much attention our way.

"I'll make sure the kitchen is aware. You aren't like most of the guests that come here."

"Yeah, hold the human flesh, please," I said without realizing I was speaking aloud.

Bastien's mouth fell open, and even Adrian's eyes grew wide with surprise. I fought the urge to wince. What kind of idiot made vampire jokes in a restaurant full of vampires? For a moment, I thought fae would be added to the evening's menu. But then Bastien broke into hysterical laughter.

"You're a funny one, girl! That's good, that's good. So that's a no to the rack of severed legs and roasted human heart, yes?"

That got them all laughing. I immediately knew why Bastien Champagne was beloved by so many worldwide. He had an easygoing nature and didn't take himself too seriously, so it was easy to forget that he was a vampire.

"I don't mean to interrupt, but there is something I would like to speak to you about, my king," Bastien said. "It will just take a minute of your precious time."

Adrian looked resignedly at Bastien and winced before rising from the table.

"Forgive me," he said apologetically. "Duty calls. I'll be right back."

"Don't go anywhere. I will only borrow this handsome fellow for a minute or two. It was a pleasure to meet such a beauty. You are most welcome in my restaurants anytime you wish. I will ensure that the kitchen takes note of your...dietary restrictions."

"I appreciate that. Thank you."

Adrian was livid with Bastien for interrupting the dinner before it had even begun, but he did his best to bite back his anger. It would have been rude to snap at him in his place of business. While Adrian technically had lordship over every building in Hell's Kitchen, he respected Bastien's role within the walls of The Belfry and his other establishments.

"Seems like a fun girl you've got down there," Bastien said as they went up the stairs to find a place to speak more privately. "And a married woman, no less. I never took you as a man who reaches for forbidden fruit, no?"

Adrian ignored him. "I would very much like to get back to her. What was so urgent that we needed to talk here and now?"

When they reached the balcony and could easily detect any prying eyes in the restaurant, Bastien leaned against the railing and let out a heavy sigh. "You know how you asked me to keep my ears out in case I heard anything?"

"Yes." Of course, Adrian remembered that.

"You know how these things go," Bastien said. He ran his hands through his long hair, playing nervously with the ponytail at the back of his head. "So far, we haven't heard much. Things have been hushed, but it's in a way that is too quiet. You know what I mean?"

"Suspicious, yes," Adrian agreed. "I got some more information myself. I stopped an attempt to sabotage another shipping truck and managed to interrogate one of the men responsible. He didn't give me much, but he did say that a vampire supplied the information."

"A vampire?" Bastien faced Adrian, looking disgusted. "One working against their own king, against their own kind? Despicable. Do you have any suspects so far?"

"I'm still trying to sort that out."

"Whenever you do, let me know so I can ensure a traitor like that never comes anywhere near my restaurants. And we won't just bounce him out of here. No, we'll chop him up and cook him, feed him to one of those guests with a particular appetite."

Bastien was always dramatic, but Adrian appreciated the sentiment. He found a certain kinship in knowing he had another person who was not afraid to go to extremes for their cause; feeding a treasonous vampire to undead cannibals was not a bad plan.

"I have a date to get back to," Adrian said, looking down at the fae woman sitting by herself at their table. She was a bright light in the darkness. Adrian noticed the other vampires glancing at Moira, certainly scenting her addictive fragrance.

She wore black jeans, a white tank top, and a red leather jacket. Her wavy hair tumbled gracefully down her shoulders and back, nearly reaching her waist. Adrian longed to run his fingers through those auburn locks, to feel their softness, to lean in and inhale the scent of fresh flowers that her hair seemed to naturally carry.

"Ah, so it is a date," Bastien said, his lips curling into a thin smile. "With a married woman, no less. And not even a vampire. Quite the scandal, but she is a beauty."

"We're in Hell's Kitchen, and I'm king. I can do whatever I want here."

"Fair enough. Well, enjoy your meal, my king." Bastien returned to his position at the railing, appearing as Lord and Master of his domain.

As Adrian descended the stairs, Bastien's gaze burned at the nape of his neck. Part of him half-expected a knife to be plunged into his back, too.

"Everything ok?" Moira looked a bit concerned.

"Just business," Adrian said.

"I didn't realize you dipped your toes into culinary enterprises."

"Oh, no, he can handle his restaurants by himself. He and I have an agreement on how we aid one another. I will say that his talents for sussing out gossip are quite handy, particularly when I need information I cannot obtain through our regular channels."

That made a lot of sense. Adrian was using Bastien's popularity and social ties to his advantage. From the little that Adrian shared, I pieced together that the restaurants weren't just for Bastien's business benefits–they were a global network of spying stations that no one suspected.

Without their knowledge, every person that went into one of Bastien Champagne's establishments fell under his watchful eye. It might have been an underhanded strategy to use people's hunger to spy on them, but it was effective and seemed harmless enough.

Adrian Sutton was much more strategic than his enemies gave him credit for. The Guardians often acted like Adrian was nothing more than a mindless monster whose obsession with blood clouded his intuition, but that could not have been further from the truth.

I needed to get to know him better, not just for the Guardians, but because I had the urge to discover everything I could about him. I wanted to understand the perspective of someone that spent centuries committing awful acts for survival.

No, I had to stay focused.

I had to make sure I learned things that would be useful to my real employers. That was what I was trained for and put in place to do.

"Are you happy, Adrian?"

Adrian couldn't hold in his laughter. It was an innocent question, but a complex one as well. "Happy? Hundreds of vampires would say it is my job to make *them* happy." He looked at Moira, losing himself for a moment in her blue-green eyes. She did not respond, letting the silence build between them, watching him intently as she waited for him to continue.

He sighed. "Am I happy? I suppose, but my happiness is not really a priority in my life. It's not always easy to do what's best for so many people. It's challenging when those people struggle every moment of every day with an insatiable hunger that demands to be satisfied. The key is to try to keep them happy and healthy while protecting the rest of the world from their eating habits, which is why someone threatening our resources is such a problem. It doesn't just make things worse for us; it puts everyone in danger."

"And you don't want that."

"Of course not. Stability keeps the world spinning."

Moira seemed surprised by his response. Adrian couldn't blame her. He knew he was seen as some terrible boogeyman by the other communities. They thought he wanted to drain everyone of their blood until the whole world drowned. He wasn't a psychopath like they all believed.

"Have you thought any more about who went after your trucks?"

"It's all I can think about lately."

"That's what I figured...so what have you determined? Anyone in particular?"

Adrian studied Moira intently as if weighing a decision. He had a suspicion, but he didn't dare speak it aloud—not in the Belfry. So instead, he nodded his head in the direction of the balcony where Bastien Champagne stood watching them. Moira seemed to understand the message. She knew better than to say anything when the spymaster had ears everywhere.

Moira cut into her food, not looking up as she whispered, making sure to be as vague as possible. "But why would he choose a different restaurant?"

Adrian did his best to keep up with her coded conversation. "Maybe he is unhappy with the current investors and thinks he could do a better job. Or perhaps he wishes to pave the way for a completely different...establishment...to take over instead."

"Do you really think he would make such a risky business decision?"

"I think it's easier to make bold moves when you have friends in high places. There are few people around that are as universally loved as him."

That was an absolute truth. Everyone enjoyed Bastien Champagne's food and company. It didn't matter where you came from or what species you were. He had a talent for knowing exactly what to say, no matter the situation. He was someone that Adrian always admired but felt he should be cautious of.

After all, Adrian might have been the king of the vampires, but he would lose to the beloved restaurateur in a popularity contest. That alone was reason enough to be wary of Bastien; that was a kind of power Adrian didn't want to be held over his head.

"I hope you're wrong."

"I hope so, too."

They enjoyed the rest of their meal, but Adrian continued sneaking glances at the vampire on the balcony, who flashed a smile when he noticed he was being watched.

CHAPTER THIRTEEN

Revelations

When they finished dinner, Moira and Adrian made their way back outside to the streets of Hell's Kitchen. It was a quiet evening thus far, and his belly was satisfied by a much different meal than he'd consumed the previous night.

"Did you have a good time?" Adrian asked.

He was happy to see her smirk. "It was okay. Food could have been better."

"Next time, you can take me to a fae eatery," Adrian offered.

"Next time?" Moira looked at him with one eyebrow raised.

"My king!" The shout came from their side, and a familiar face ran toward them. It was Felicia Lorne who, evidently, had not left town as Adrian asked. He was in no mood for another argument with her.

However, she didn't look like she was there to debate. Instead, she looked like she had just run across the city to find him.

"Sire, you need to come with me. Immediately. Another of our red rigs has been attacked. Hurry! This way!"

Adrian didn't stop to ask questions as his rage catapulted him into action. He moved to follow Felicia, taking Moira's hand to bring her along. Adrian couldn't believe someone would still attempt to mess with his operations after the carnage of the night before. He was tempted to take off into the night sky and rain hell upon his enemies, but he was concerned about leaving Moira alone.

As they followed Felicia down an alleyway, Adrian called, "What the bloody hell happened?"

"Some of our evening trucks were hit simultaneously. Whoever is doing this just caused massive damage!"

"Can we all just stop for a second?" Moira asked as she grabbed Felicia's arm. The vampire glared in fury at the fae for daring to touch her, but under her king's scrutiny, Felicia did not pull away. Moira's face contorted in confusion as she chewed her bottom lip. "The trucks were attacked?"

Felicia nodded. "Yes, that's what I just said!" she snapped.

Moira stared at Felicia for a moment and then turned back to Adrian.

In an almost monotone voice, as if puzzle pieces were coming together in her mind, Moira said, "She's lying."

Her words were like a punch to the gut. Adrian didn't understand. "What?"

Moira stared unwaveringly at Felicia. Her brow furrowed, and she clenched her teeth. She was utterly focused on the vampire. Then, suddenly, Moira let go of Felicia and took a protective step backward toward Adrian. "You shouldn't have answered my question. You might have convinced him, but you can't lie to me."

Adrian eyed Moira. Fae could not be deceived; this was a fact he knew. But it was not one that Felicia would have necessarily recalled. She was too busy traveling for work and wasn't used to speaking with a fae regularly. As Adrian's scrutiny settled on Felicia, the shock of her mistake ghosted across her face before she regained her composure.

"How dare you," she hissed at Moira. "I am not lying!"

"Really? Because you just lied again." Moira took Adrian's arm and stepped back, trying to pull him away. Her gaze didn't leave Felicia, not even for a second.

Adrian didn't budge. He needed answers, and the only way to get them was to sort it out right then and there. He looked at Moira. "Are you absolutely certain?"

"I'd bet my life on it," Moira said.

"You can't seriously be listening to this fae's accusations, Adrian," Felicia said, looking noticeably flustered. "You can't believe the poison she's feeding you! She's just trying to turn you against your own kind!"

"You know I'm not," Moira whispered. "You have to trust me."

"I have served you for hundreds of years. I have been your friend since we met on the deck of the *Annabelle*. My loyalty has never wavered. I've more than proven myself. Surely my word means more than some wood nymph you barely know?"

Maybe it should have. Perhaps it made more sense to trust Felicia, considering their history—but that very history kept him from putting his faith in a fellow vampire. Their past had been filled with frustration, animosity, and a good deal of resentment. Felicia had stuck with him for centuries, but in all those years, she often felt more like a rival than a friend.

Moira had shown him more kindness in a few short months than Felicia had managed in hundreds of years. There had to be a good reason for that. It had to mean something.

Felicia grew impatient. "You can't be serious, Adrian! After everything—"

It was time to pick a side. Adrian glanced at Moira and decided to follow his instincts. He trusted one of them much more than the other. He turned back to Felicia, who was practically ready to bare her fangs.

"You keep talking about how we have known each other for so long, for hundreds of years. And you're right. We have worked together for lifetimes. So, tell me...after centuries, why have you decided to conspire against me?"

The words seemed to strike her in the face. She dropped the act, and her signature look of superiority returned as she narrowed her eyes at Adrian. In those few seconds, Adrian knew without question that she was the one who had betrayed him.

Felicia giggled. "Why? Maybe you are not the great ruler you imagine yourself to be. Maybe your sovereignty has more than reached its expiration date."

"My rule is for eternity," Adrian countered.

"Ideally, you could make that happen, but a vampire's immortality is not guaranteed. One must tread carefully in this world...and you have made so many mistakes. Working with forest children like her, for instance." Felicia jerked her chin toward Moira.

Adrian quickly glanced at Moira, and Felicia took full advantage of the distraction. Moving with vamp speed, she backhanded Moira.

The power of the blow sent Moira flying toward the wall of the alley, and her head slammed against the brick wall, knocking her unconscious. A bolt of fury shot through Adrian, and he bared his fangs at Felicia while listening closely to ensure he could still hear Moira's heartbeat.

"You will die for this," he snarled as he moved to place himself between Moira and Felicia.

His positioning wasn't lost on Felicia, and a calculating smile crossed her face. She was a brilliant strategist, and Adrian knew better than to underestimate her.

"There he is. King Adrian Sutton—the petulant child who acts in his own favor instead of doing what is best for all vampires. You forget how much time I spend in other parts of the world. And do you know what I hear? Discontent. Bitterness. Anger. There are many who spit on your name and your rule. They aren't just whispers, either. People voice their frustration with anyone who will listen. They shout it in the streets. There is so much resentment building, and you refuse to hear it. You are fine to sit in Hell's Kitchen, in this echo chamber where you think you are some beloved monarch."

"I don't concern myself with the opinions of people like that—"

"Well, you should. Those voices matter. You gave me the job of ensuring that our global interests are strong and stable. I have done that job for hundreds of years, and the greatest threat I have encountered is you. That is just a fact. If you remain our king, the rest of the world will end up at our gates. We can't fight the whole world, Adrian."

"But you think you can do better?"

"Of course I can," Felicia said with certainty. "I actually know what's going on out there. I care. That is what separates us. You turn a blind eye to anything outside Hell's Kitchen's borders. Sure, you have people like me keep track of it for you, but you really couldn't care less."

Adrian laughed at the irony of being reprimanded by Felicia; she was the one who had gone out of her way to hurt their people. She didn't recognize just how hypocritical she was being. She obviously deemed her actions justifiable.

Felicia Lorne had always been ambitious, but he never thought she would try to take his throne by force.

"You know, a part of me has been suspicious of you for hundreds of years. Obviously, you wanted more, but I figured you wanted to be my queen or something along those lines. I never imagined that you wanted to wear the crown yourself."

"I'm sure you couldn't imagine it," Felicia said venomously. "Your pride and ego make it impossible for you to comprehend the idea of vampires not wanting to follow your every command. You were so focused on your enemies outside of Hell's Kitchen. The Guardians. The Usurpers. Surely one of them was trying to weaken us. No vampire would go after their own blood supply, right? No vampire would dare turn on their beloved king, right? I wasn't worried about that. I knew you would find a way to replenish it. I just wanted you shaken, drawn out into the open. I couldn't exactly do this in your office."

"You shouldn't be doing it at all. You swore an oath."

"I stayed true to that oath for centuries! And in the end, I watched you grow complacent. Your kingdom is stagnant. I upheld your wishes in a changing world, and you haven't even noticed."

"So, you are going to assassinate me? You think your problems will suddenly vanish? We both know that that is shortsighted, Felicia. My supporters won't stand for it. They would not give credence to your ridiculous claim."

"You underestimate how much influence I have within your organization. I would have the backing of all our international branches. I have extensive knowledge of our enemies and a good relationship with most of the members of the Council. I think I would make a fine candidate for the crown. It would fit my head much better than it has ever fit yours."

Adrian was suddenly back on the *Annabelle* where he and Felicia first encountered one another. He'd thought he found a kindred spirit. That was when they had been moving toward the same destination, but now it was clear they weren't even sailing the same sea anymore. They probably hadn't been for a very long time.

"Do you remember when we first met? Do you remember the sway of that ship? I wish I had seen it then."

"Seen what?"

"Just how delusional you are."

Felicia let out a roar and rushed him, drawing a wooden stake. He had seen others defend themselves against her, but he didn't understand her power, not until that moment. She was ferocious and came at him like a cannonball. He grabbed her wrist, but her speed and strength forced them both to the ground.

Felicia was nearly as old and powerful as Adrian. It didn't help that she had taken him by surprise. There wasn't enough of a difference in their strength to level the playing field, especially not when she had the advantage of much better leverage.

"I told you. Like so many rulers before you, you have gotten lazy. You have been idle for far too long while I have done nothing but prepare for this. I knew for decades that this had to be done. The key was getting you into a vulnerable position. So now here you are, in the dirt where you belong!" Felicia's fangs hovered above his face, and her hot saliva dripped onto his cheek.

Adrian grimaced as the stake drew closer to his chest, ready to puncture his heart. He couldn't hold it at bay much longer. He stared at the sharpened piece of wood that threatened to snuff out the eternal flame of his life. Everything around him fell silent.

"You have lived long enough. No king should rule forever. Change can only happen when new blood is allowed a chance. It is time for your reign to end. Our people will be better for it."

Adrian ignored her taunts. He put all his energy into keeping the stake away from him.

"Stop!" Moira limped toward them.

Felicia chuckled at the sight of her, and she certainly didn't stop. "Oh look, your little fae whore. She is further validation that there needs to be a change. A disgusting creature like her has no business being anywhere near us. So, after I've watched you turn to ash, I will drain every drop of her blood and leave her here to rot. After all, this is your precious Hell's Kitchen, and rats will feast on her body!"

"Let. Him. Go," Moira growled.

"I'll be with you in a moment, girl," Felicia hissed. "Before you die, you can witness the most important event in the history of vampirism. The king's death will change everything for the better, but neither of you will be around to see it."

Adrian stared at the stake's point. His hands quivered as he tried to stop it, but his defense was about to crumble.

Felicia leaned in close and whispered, "Now it ends, sweet Adrian. I will serve our people well."

The wooden stake breached his chest, breaking through the skin. The pain that accompanied it was unlike anything he had ever felt. It was worse than he had ever imagined. The deeper the weapon burrowed into him, the more his heart burned, and he could feel his immortality slipping away.

He couldn't stop his roar of agony. He had spent so long laying the groundwork for his kingdom, building it into something vital. It would fall apart without him; he had no doubt about that, especially if Felicia Lorne was the one who took his place. Her unquenchable thirst for world domination would mean the end of the vampire seethe as he'd built it. She would cause a global war that the vampires could not win.

Adrian thought back to when he first turned, the start of his new life, and the promise of eternity. Except now, he was facing true death.

The tip of the wooden stake poked his heart. Death itself had found him, ending his reign forever. He glanced over at Moira Collins. He wanted his last memory to be something beautiful.

Moira flung her hand toward Felicia and let out a cry. "No!"

The stake in Felicia's hand warped and changed. The wood sprouted branches that burst through her fingers, elongating into thin spears that took on a life of their own. They stretched backward and buried themselves in Felicia Lorne's chest.

The vampire's eyes grew wide with horror. She hadn't had time to prepare herself for the end before it reached her. The branches that sprouted from the stake had impaled her directly through the heart. In her final moments, as she looked down at the pieces of wood piercing her skin, she must have felt foolish. She'd forgotten about Moira's power, or maybe she didn't think anyone would go out of their way to save Adrian.

Felicia's skin turned gray and cracked, but she mustered up the energy to break the stake lodged in Adrian's heart. She wheezed, "If you think my death will end the uprising, you are a fool. You have no idea how many have already betrayed you. You cannot stop what is coming."

Her final gaze fell on Moira. She looked at her with pity and disappointment. "He is going to be the death of you, girl. He is going to be the death of everyone...."

Flames burst from the vampire's wounded heart, and Felicia Lorne was burned away.

Adrian laid there and waited for those same flames to come for him, too.

CHAPTER FOURTEEN

Life and Undeath

I t was strange to watch an immortal life come to an end, knowing I was the reason behind it.

Adrian lay on his back, choking. The shock of killing Felicia had left me frozen for a moment, but his pained gasps shook me out of my stupor. I must not have stopped Felicia in time, after all.

I hurried over to him and crouched at his side, lifting the back of his head. He stared up at me, and it was the first time I had ever seen Adrian Sutton look afraid.

I put my hand over the wound and channeled my power, but something stopped me. Adrian's death might be good for the Guardians, and our mission would finally be over. If the vampire monarch was dead, we could go back to our lives. If the great evil that worried the Guardians so much was gone, we would finally be free. Then again, another vampire, a much worse one than Adrian, could assume power.

Adrian coughed up more blood as his face turned gray. He stared up at me with expectation and confusion in his eyes. He had hired me to heal vampires, and I was not using my power to save their king.

"Moira," he rasped. He was fading, and at any moment, his heart would give out. His undead body would erupt in flames, just like Felicia. His eyes flickered.

It didn't matter what everyone else thought about Adrian Sutton. I had spent enough time with him to see that he wasn't some monster who spent his days torturing puppies and plotting world domination. Instead, he was an eternal survivor who cared for his people.

Dustin and the Guardians would disapprove, but I couldn't watch him die.

I pushed my power into his wound to repair the damage the stake had done to his heart. I used my magic to gently pull the wood from his body. His graying skin regained color and the hole in his chest shrank as if nothing had ever penetrated it. As my power completely enveloped him in its warmth, the vampire king's eyes opened as if he was being reborn.

"Moira," he whispered.

Adrian sat up and looked down at his bloody clothes. He appeared to be in shock as he realized he was no longer dying on the cobblestones. He let out a long exhale of relief before his gaze flicked to me. He smiled.

"Are you alright?" I asked quietly.

For a moment, I had wondered if I was too late. If I'd been there, only feet away, unable to save him, I'm not sure I would ever be able to forgive myself.

"I think so," Adrian said, still holding his chest. He tapped different parts of his torso to check if any holes needed to be plugged. "Yeah, I think I'm okay. Let's get out of this alley, shall we?" He climbed to his feet and reached for my hand, smiling sheepishly as he did so.

Wiping a hand across his well-muscled bottom, Adrian sucked in a long breath before letting it out, apparently relishing that he could do such a simple thing. He looked at me, and I saw something soft in his awe-filled eyes. At that moment, Adrian Sutton wasn't some legendary vampire king, or the monster many claimed him to be. Instead, he was a person who had cheated true death, and he appreciated the life he still had.

"Thank—"

I instinctively threw my hand over his mouth to stop him.

"Don't," I said. "You can't thank me, remember?"

Adrian nodded and I slowly removed my hand from his mouth. He glanced at my blood-covered palm. Then, he stared at me for so long that I began to feel uncomfortable, but I couldn't look away.

"Fine," he whispered with a smile. "I won't."

Those intense brown eyes bore into my soul as the vampire king lifted a hesitant hand toward my face. My lids closed of their own volition as he gently brushed a few stray curls across my forehead, settling them behind my ear. I didn't know when the tears began, but they burned against my cheeks; reminders of the horrible trauma we'd just experienced.

Adrian cupped my cheek and wiped a tear with his thumb. Then, in a moment that felt like time itself had ceased, his lips crashed onto mine.

My knees buckled and I sank into Adrian, resting my hands against his crimson-stained chest. The sheer power of his kiss was like nothing I'd ever experienced.

Some claimed that vampires did not have souls, but I begged to differ. Adrian's kiss allowed our hearts to merge, and as warmth and power filled my chest, I was convinced that the king of the vampires was baring his soul to me.

At that moment, I forgot who and what I was. It didn't matter that I was a fae and Adrian was a vampire. It didn't matter that he was one of the most dangerous people on the planet or that my purpose for being in his life was to spy for the Guardians. My marriage to Dustin was irrelevant. Nothing held substance except the feeling sweeping through me—and I eagerly kissed him back.

When he pulled away, he stared into my eyes with an unspoken vow on his face.

"I hope that conveys how much I appreciate what you did for me," Adrian said carefully. "And whether or not I say the words, know that I am in your debt forever." At that moment, the centuries-old being who stood before me offered me a sweeping, regal bow.

"No," I insisted. "You don't owe me anything—"

"I do," Adrian said, stepping back as his expression hardened. "And I give you my solemn vow that I will make it up to you, but there are things I need to take care of first. What she did...." He shook his head as he looked over at Felicia Lorne's ashes. "There are some conversations I need to have with my people, and time is of the essence."

"Of course," I said. Adrian had been betrayed, and he nearly died as a result. He needed time to think. I waved a hand at him and said, "Go do whatever you have to. I'll be around."

"You always are," Adrian said with a smile. "I'm glad you came to us. I don't know what we'd do without you—what *I* would do without you. And...I'm sorry about...if I was too...I probably shouldn't have done that..." he nodded toward my face, his eyes glued to mine.

I waved my hand, brushing away his worry despite my confusion about what had happened. "It's okay! Really! Just go talk to your friends and clear this whole thing up! Well, not this thing—" I awkwardly motioned toward my lips and my cheeks started to burn. Then, trying to salvage my frazzled ramblings, I pointed to the ash pile. "Clear that whole thing up."

"Of course," Adrian said. "Of course. I will have it all sorted. You should get back to Dustin; he is probably worried. Come, I will escort you home."

Adrian's words stung. We had just shared the kiss of a lifetime, and now he was sending me back home to my husband. Unfortunately, he was right; I needed to go.

"What? Oh, um, no. I'll be fine, thank you."

Adrian considered me for a moment, then nodded curtly. He stepped backward, then, in a blur, he was gone. I stood, staring at the empty space before me, and even with all the confusion running through my mind, I knew with absolute certainty that I would much rather have remained in that cold, dirty alley with the king of all vampires.

CHAPTER FIFTEEN

Judas is Dead

Adrian didn't take much time to get Felicia's ashes into an urn. They had plenty in stock at the compound. One never knew when they would need to have a funeral for a fallen ally. But, of course, Felicia would not be given that kind of honor; she didn't deserve one after her betrayal. The members of his inner circle needed to gather to discuss her deception, but no one would give any heartfelt eulogies.

He immediately sent out a summons for all the members of his inner circle and stressed that Bastien Champagne was expected to attend. He wanted to personally look them all in the eye to gauge their reactions to the news.

After a quick shower, Adrian walked toward his office with Felicia's urn in hand. He considered what he would say to the Council, but images of Moira kept interrupting his train of thought. Adrian knew his precise reason for the kiss, and it was more than just a show of appreciation. He had wanted to do that for a very long time. He never expected her to kiss him back, though.

There was something between them that no words could describe. Adrian had taken many lovers in the centuries he'd been alive. Beautiful women from across the globe had shared his bed, but no one had ever elicited the feelings or experiences he had when he was with Moira. That kiss...he needed to stop thinking about it. His body began to react noticeably and now was not the time or place.

He shook his head, trying desperately to redirect his thoughts. He needed to address the problem at hand, and he could reflect upon whatever was happening between him and his fae healer later.

When Adrian pushed open the doors to his office, he found the usual suspects standing around the room. Royce lingered by the desk with his arms crossed over his chest. He glanced at his watch and scowled as Adrian strode in. Kellan leaned back in one of the chairs, looking much less nervous than he had during the last meeting; the fact he didn't have to deliver bad news this time seemed to have lifted his spirits. Augustus Pope examined some of Adrian's library books on one wall with mild interest.

Bastien Champagne was notably absent from the room. That wasn't surprising, but it was bothersome.

The Council came to attention when Adrian placed the urn on his desk. Their focus fell on the object, and they all looked at each other questioningly. Adrian was just about to give them some context when the door opened, and Bastien Champagne appeared.

"Sorry I'm late," he said. "Was hosting a rather voracious troll in the Upper West Side. It took everything I had to pull myself away. It's been so long I almost forgot the directions to get here." Bastien flashed the Council a wide grin.

"It's good to have ya' back here," Kellan nodded. "I hope biz'ness is well."

Bastien ran a hand through his tied-back hair, ensuring he looked presentable. "Oh yes, my friend, business is booming, as always."

"We have some business of our own," Adrian said sharply and shot Bastien a look that made it clear he wasn't happy with his tardiness. "If you don't mind, that is."

Bastien laid a hand on his chest and bowed slightly, then filed in, taking a seat beside Kellan. They all brought their undivided attention back to the urn on the desk. Augustus, in particular, eyed it apprehensively, running his hand nervously across his chin. Considering his job was keeping track of vampires and vampire recruits, he knew very well what the urn meant.

"While it's nice to have Bastien attend one of these gatherings for once, you may have noticed we are missing someone." Everyone nodded, and Adrian did his best to disguise his fury. Fortunately, they all seemed too focused on the urn to notice, and he could see the realization begin to click in their minds.

"Well, as you have probably guessed, Felicia Lorne technically is still present. Right here." He tapped the top of the urn with his palm and sighed disappointedly.

Adrian carefully watched the grim faces of his Council members, studying them to see if any of them would betray anything; they did not. Kellan's Irish temper erupted. "She's dead!? What the feck happened!? Don't tell me it was those bastards that hit our trucks!"

"In a way...since she was the one that helped those 'bastards' find our trucks to begin with. The nutter planned the whole thing, in an attempt to assume the throne for herself. Then, when I stopped the attacks, she tried another approach. She attempted to assassinate me."

Royce stepped in to check on him, but Adrian waved him away. "I'm perfectly fine. She tried to drive a stake through my heart, but I emerged unscathed."

He left out Moira's role in the attack. They didn't need to hear any of those details. Not only would they judge him for relying on a fae to rescue him, but some might even want Moira's head for daring to kill one of the oldest vampires in their organization. It was wiser to omit any of that from the tale. Still, Royce's cold, icy gaze seemed to dissect Adrian where he stood.

"As it turns out, we may not be as secure as I thought we were, and the attack on our blood shipments might be the start of something much worse. From what this traitorous prat told me...there is some discontentment with our regime outside this neighborhood. Possibly even whispers of mutiny and revolt. I wanted to make you all aware of the seriousness of the situation. I don't believe it ends with Felicia."

The silence in the room was so thick one could cut it with a knife. Adrian studied each Council member, noting how their gazes darted around to each other, suspicion haunting their eyes. Adrian wondered if it was due to guilt or fear.

Although it was not his intention, Adrian's announcement had successfully pitted every Council member against each other. Mistrust was a massive factor in vampire politics, and now that they were aware of the possible traitors among them, they would be second-guessing everyone.

"I will put a hold on all recruitment," Augustus said, breaking the silence. "A ban. If anyone turns a human into one of us, we will punish them for conspiring to build a rebel army."

It wasn't a bad idea, and Adrian appreciated how quickly Augustus wished to improve their situation. That was the kind of initiative they needed in all aspects of their work.

"That's a good start," Adrian said. "I want us to tread carefully in the days ahead. We need to find these weeds of dissent and pluck them before they are overgrown and it's too late. Bastien, I expect you will be even more attentive to the people entering your establishments."

"Of course," Bastien said. "If I hear even the slightest whisper about any of this, I will let you know."

"Thank you." Adrian continued to study the faces of the people in the room. He had known them for so long, and he would usually trust them with his life, but he would never make that mistake again. Unfortunately, just like Felicia, one of them might be conspiring against him at that very moment. "That's all. Please be careful out there."

They slowly cleared the room, leaving only the vampire king and his adviser.

"My apologies, my king," Royce said once they were all gone. His voice was as deep and smooth as ever, but Adrian could hear the genuine regret that laced his words. "I should have seen what she was. I should have known what she planned to do when I drank her blood."

"It's alright," Adrian said. "We know your power is not impossible to block by other means. My main concern is that others have been hiding their agendas as Felicia did. It's hard to trust anyone now."

"I will do better. Perhaps I can take more blood when someone enters, more than just a few drops," Royce said. "And you always have me, my king. Always."

"I appreciate that," Adrian said. "And I know."

As was typical, his adviser still had more he wished to say.

"However, sire...I couldn't help but notice." He pointed to Adrian's damp hair and freshly donned clothing. He knew well that his king did not shower and change clothing after a simple dinner date. "Felicia was a powerful vampire whose strength rivaled your own. She did more damage than you could admit, didn't she?"

There was no use trying to hide it from Royce. He was a very observant individual. He didn't need to pry into Adrian's memories to be able to tell at least part of what happened.

"She did."

"And the girl?"

Adrian turned to his adviser. "Girl?"

"That fae girl...Moira Collins...you were out with her when this happened, no? I do hope she is alright."

"She is fine," Adrian said. "No harm came to her."

"And she made sure no harm came to you, too, didn't she?" Royce asked. "Felicia Lorne didn't miss when she wanted someone dead. And it might have helped to have a fae on standby who could repair any wounds you were dealt. I hope you didn't thank her."

"I didn't."

Royce gave a thin smile. "Good. You can't get too close to that fae."

At least he didn't know how close they had really gotten that night.

"I won't."

CHAPTER SIXTEEN

Potential

I didn't even know if I could look at Dustin. Of course, our marriage was a performance, but there had to be times when we could be ourselves. The union we shared wasn't real—we both knew that.

So why did I feel so guilty about a kiss with another man?

Dustin was asleep when I got home, and I didn't bother waking him. I hoped I would figure out what to say to him by morning. I didn't plan to mention the kiss. That would just upset him.

Thankfully, I'd accumulated critical knowledge I could share with the Guardians. The strife among the vampires and the attempted assassination was valuable information. The Guardians underestimated Adrian, but I was uncomfortable offering details that could help them move against him. I would have to be vague and cryptic, giving them just enough to not question my loyalty—as if I even knew where my commitment was at this point.

I couldn't protect bloodsucking vampires. They were monsters. But I did want to shield the greatest of them in whatever way I could.

He was not the demon the Guardians and so many others believed him to be, and what would happen if someone far more dangerous and power-hungry than Adrian assumed control of the seethe? Should that happen, Adrian was the least of the Guardians' worries. I knew that much for certain.

As I was getting ready to climb into bed, a shadow fell across my window. Startled, I looked over and gasped as I saw the king of the vampires floating in mid-air outside my apartment building. He waved for me to come outside, and not wanting Dustin to wake, I did so as quietly as possible. Then, standing in the cold air of the early morning, I watched Adrian descend until he was standing right in front of me.

"What are you doing here?" I urgently whispered, glancing back toward the door.

"I handled what I had to with the others...and I wanted to make sure you made it home safely."

"As you can see, I did!" I said, sounding exasperated, but I was terrified my husband was going to see. Real marriage or not, it was wrong to do...whatever this was...behind his back.

"Good," Adrian said. "About what happened—"

Holding up a hand, I cut him off. He didn't need to explain. "You wanted to thank me without actually thanking me, that's all. I get it."

"It wasn't just about that," Adrian said. "I just...I would like to show you my thanks again. Many more times."

My heart pounded in my chest as I asked, "What are you saying?"

"I'm saying that I...really appreciate...that you are in my life. I know you're married, and this is somewhat untoward, but I have walked this world for a long time, Moira. I can safely say that I've never... bloody hell...what I'm trying to say is...when you showed me the potential of life on that roof...everything changed."

I nodded my agreement. "It did."

"Life isn't always exactly how you plan or want it to be, and I have spent centuries building something, brick by brick, and I'm still not satisfied. I need someone who can show me another way. I couldn't bring out the best in those plants, but you could. You are the person I need by my side."

His words were more passionate than any I'd ever heard from another man. It was messy and clumsy, but it was real. A king who was supposed to be a monster was speaking to me as a person, exposing his vulnerabilities and deepest desires.

They were all wrong about him. Every last one of them.

Adrian Sutton was not a demon. He was an immortal, yes; he was a sinner, a savior, a frightened boy, a brave man, a vicious killer, a gentle caretaker, a vampire, and a king, all rolled into one ugly, beautiful being.

I had heard enough. Right there in the street, I kissed the ruler of the vampires again. This time, neither of us pulled away. We were back on that rooftop, surrounded by the beauty of mortality and life.

Unfortunately, even Adrian couldn't stay there forever.

The morning mists surrounded us as the sun began its slow ascent over Hell's Kitchen, and I knew, beyond a shadow of a doubt, that Sir Adrian Sutton had just made my life much, much more complicated. *Crap.*

THE END

Vampsire – Chapter One

1 982 – Hell's Kitchen, NYC

That kiss. It was desperate, frenzied, and seething with fiery passion. It was a clash of two worlds, reverberating through the barren alleyway of Hell's Kitchen. It was a deafening roar that threatened to engulf me in its flames, and I could not free my racing mind from its all-consuming embrace.

Four days ago, I kissed Sir Adrian Sutton—the king of all vampires—and it was like lightning striking my veins, brilliant and terrifying. Both of us had been soaked in blood as we stood solemnly beside the pile of ashes that were the remains of Felicia Lorne, Adrian's former cohort turned traitor. That kiss represented more than just a passionate moment; it held a thousand unspoken words of revenge and fury.

As a 312-year-old fae with the god-borne powers of my ancestors, I knew my people and vampires were natural enemies. My magic was comprised of light and life, while vampire magic was fueled by darkness and death. I should not have lost myself in that kiss or in the vampire who would not leave my thoughts. I shouldn't have reveled in sharing something so intimate with the greatest of them—or perhaps the worst of them—but that was the truth of it.

I worked as an undercover spy for a global faction of supernaturals known as the Guardians. The primary directive of the Guardians was to protect humanity from their mortal enemies, the Usurpers. Their secondary edict was to work with the human governments to prevent the masses from discovering that supernaturals existed.

The war between the Guardians and the Usurpers began in 10,000 B.C., when the Usurpers, a group of power-hungry supernaturals, decided humans were vermin and needed to be eradicated from the planet. The Usurpers' army boasted some of the deadliest and most evil preternatural beings in existence. The Guardians were the only coalition with the numbers, magic, and resources to keep them at bay.

The vampire seethe, under its reigning monarch, Sir Adrian Sutton, was the lynchpin between the Guardians and the Usurpers. During his 600 years of immortality, Adrian built an international kingdom of vampires and established a network of powerful allies and spies.

Adrian chose to keep his seethe out of the war between the Guardians and the Usurpers, but if he ever decided to ally with one, it would be a turning point in the battle.

I left the fae realm over a hundred years ago after our land was decimated by invaders. During the spring equinox, fae folk can pass between realms using magical portals as gateways to other lands.

I chose Earth because two of my cousins were Guardians on this planet, and they assured me I could seek sanctuary with them if I ever needed to.

I couldn't protect my kin from slaughter, so I decided to become a soldier for those I *could* help: humans. I trained for a decade with the Guardians before being assigned an undercover position as a spy within the vampire seethe.

Five years ago, a confidential informant for the Guardians reported that Adrian Sutton was looking for a healer to work full-time at his headquarters in Hell's Kitchen, so I was the natural choice for infiltration.

The Guardians arranged a false cover story, including a fake husband—my coworker, Dustin Collins. As a cheetah shifter, Dustin was planted by the Guardians as an enforcer for Adrian.

Everyone at the vampire seethe believed Dustin and I were legally married and in love, but our marriage was only for show. I had no romantic feelings for Dustin, but sadly, he did not feel the same.

When Dustin and I were initially tasked with spying on the vampire monarch, the Guardians described Adrian as a sadistic, wrathful, and savage beast. However, our interactions painted a different picture.

Of course, he was dangerous and intimidating, but no more than most leaders. Furthermore, he was not someone who enjoyed hurting innocent people. Adrian did what was necessary for the survival of his business and community, but he did not live to inflict pain and suffering on others.

The same night we kissed, Felicia Lorne had said he was too soft and weak to be their king. She then tried to assassinate him—which I prevented.

I realized it didn't matter what other people thought of Adrian. Most of them had never met him or even attempted to understand him. So who were they to judge and condemn him?

If Felicia Lorne's coup attempt had not been thwarted, she would have claimed Adrian's kingdom. Felicia intended to seize control on a global scale, assuring all-out war amongst the factions who held power.

Adrian was no such monster. In fact, he was the best vampire leader the Guardians could hope for.

I took a deep breath and shook my head to clear my thoughts. I had work to do, and I needed to focus.

Beatrix Boyd was one of the vampires I had grown to care for in the compound. She greeted me with her signature warmth, showing no animosity toward my fae heritage. Beatrix took the time to get to know me instead of treating me like an outcast because of my race. Her blue eyes would grow round with wonder, and she'd softly gasp each time I used my power to heal someone.

She told me she was turned during the Great Depression, and her life became much better once she was a vampire. Despite being born at the turn of the century, she still looked like a bubbly young woman with her blonde hair tied back in a ponytail.

"I suppose there isn't much for you to do here with no injured soldiers to treat."

She was right. "Yeah . . . things have been slow ever since the attacks on the blood trucks stopped . . ."

Beatrix beamed. "That's right. The whole compound has been buzzing with rumors about what happened."

I feigned nonchalance and asked, "What do you mean?" to conceal my looming curiosity.

Beatrix hesitated, knowing she shouldn't reveal the information. "I'm not sure I should tell you this, especially since you're . . ."

"Not a vampire?" I laughed. "It's alright to tell me," I assured her. "I won't tell anyone else, I promise. You don't have to share if you don't want to, though."

She glanced around furtively before leaning closer. "Rumor has it that Felicia Lorne instigated the attacks on the red rigs to overthrow Adrian and take charge herself."

I played my part as convincingly as possible. Only Adrian and I were aware that I had witnessed Felicia's act of treason. The truth of the event was meant to stay hidden, so I put on a show to make it look like I was just as stunned as everyone else. I widened my eyes and let out an exaggerated gasp to appear wholly taken aback.

Beatrix nodded and flashed a mischievous smile. "Yes. It's all people have been talking about. Adrian showed Kellan an urn full of Felicia's ashes in his office."

When he heard the news, Kellan Fallon wasted no time spreading Adrian's secrets to all who would listen. Though he was over four centuries old and one of Adrian's council members, his youthful, gregarious nature meant he often got ahead of himself, unable to resist sharing juicy tales.

Beatrix shifted nervously in her seat, and her gaze flitted from the office door to my face. She wore a wary expression, and she spoke in a hushed tone. "You need to keep this between us. Don't tell anyone, and don't let on that you heard it from me."

"My lips are sealed." I meant it. I did not need to spread rumors. Instead, I wanted to find out how reliable the gossip was concerning Felicia Lorne and Adrian Sutton. I needed to discover if it matched up with what I already knew.

Chapter Two

Adrian Sutton had lived for six centuries, and in all his years, he'd never paused for a moment of indecision. He was a man who carefully crafted his plans and actions. He often consulted Royce, his most trusted counselor, and contemplated every possible factor before proceeding. Spontaneous and impulsive behavior wasn't part of his nature.

Kissing Moira Collins was not something he had planned for. He had been with many women before, always consensually, and his reputation as a British gentleman had never been questioned. But Moira was different. She was a fae, and he could feel something stirring in his cold, dead heart—something that he had never experienced before.

Adrian kept telling himself that his feelings couldn't get in the way of his responsibilities. He had to remain solid and emotionless as the ruler of his kingdom, but he couldn't shake his growing affections.

It was impossible to ignore their strong connection, no matter how much he tried.

Whenever Adrian was close to Moira, he couldn't help but stare in her direction. He was drawn to the infinite depths of her blue-green eyes and the fire of her vibrant red hair. Her body moved with grace, radiating a brightness that seemed to come from the depths of her soul. Everything about her was perfect.

Her scent filled his lungs like pure oxygen, carrying the essence of the forest and soft pine needles glistening with morning dew. He felt as though every ounce of his being was aflame in her presence, and he'd never be able to quench the fire she lit inside him.

Her voice wafted around him like a warm breeze. Her words carried a hint of an Irish lilt, exotic and sweet. She displaced the cobwebs that clung to his dark soul.

Adding to the complexity of their situation, Adrian owed Moira the most significant debt of all—his life. At the time of his assassination attempt, his emotions were a whirlwind. He had never been so close to death as when Moira used her magic to save him. The pain of Felicia Lorne's stake as it entered his heart would remain with him always; it nearly ended his immortality, after all.

Adrian tried, unsuccessfully, to convince himself that the kiss he shared with Moira was simply an expression of appreciation. But he and Moira both knew it was more than that. The vampire king had initiated the kiss, but she quickly reciprocated. Over the years, Moira had become one of his closest friends and confidants; increasingly,

Adrian preferred her company to the vampires with whom he usually spent time.

Adrian's thoughts were on Moira as he stood in the center of his office with the other vampires of his inner circle. The Council had recently been thrown off balance by the defection of Felicia Lorne, and they were still trying to recover—both on a practical basis and emotionally.

Adrian's mentor and closest adviser, Royce, wore a perennial scowl. He had been changed into a vampire in his fifties, and his age was apparent. Royce paused in contemplation as he ran a hand over his wrinkled skin. "It's been an eventful few days," he said. "And not just for you, sire. Felicia was at the very center of our organization before she tried to snatch your throne away. As an international liaison, her role in the seethe was absolutely essential."

Adrian gave a slight nod in agreement. As usual, Royce was right on target. He continued, "She kept things running smoothly abroad—or so she claimed. Now that she's gone, it's up to us to ensure our relations with other countries don't suffer."

Kellan Fallon gave a slight shrug, showing his usual indifference. Despite his long life, his mental age was still that of a young adult, and he tended to be easily distracted. He needed to focus more on the conversation. "Wasn't that Felicia's responsibility?"

Adrian sighed, knowing he'd have to go over it again for Kellan. "Bloody hell, Kellan. She obviously can't finish that assignment now," he said, gesturing to the vase of ashes on his desk. "Her death has had a ripple effect across our operation, and those we're in contact with will be demanding answers. She was the one who managed our relationships with vampires outside the city and other supernatural species. We must move quickly to appoint someone new to maintain our alliances worldwide."

He turned to Augustus Pope, who was responsible for recruitment within their organization. If anyone knew who was qualified to serve as a capable replacement for Felicia Lorne, it would be Augustus.

Augustus's brown eyes opened wide, shining brightly amid flawless ebony skin as he realized the Council waited for him to speak. He rubbed his bald head as if trying to massage a good thought into existence.

"Several people might be suitable . . . I can put together a pool of candidates. But in the meantime, what would you like to do?" His eyes landed on Adrian; the black of his pupils gleamed beneath the overhead lights in the Council chamber like onyx stones washed in sunlight.

Adrian contemplated the situation. It had been centuries since a vampire had needed to be replaced in their position of authority, and the current dilemma posed quite a challenge. He scanned the faces in the room, searching for someone to appoint.

The fact was, no one could assume Felicia's responsibilities because they all had essential duties of their own. He realized he had no choice but to take matters into his own hands. As king, he had to take action. "Looks like I'm the one for the job—for now, at least."

Royce's eyes flashed with rage. "That is absurd! Felicia had to traverse dangerous terrain where vampires barely had a foothold. Stepping outside of Hell's Kitchen invites a whole world of risks. What you are considering . . . abandoning this city to attend to our far-flung affairs . . . the thought is preposterous! You might as well extend a hand of invitation to your enemies, granting them license to end your reign with a single blow. No! A king's place is at his stronghold, lest he risks his life and power!"

Adrian glared, his face thunderous. He clenched his fists, the muscles in his arms straining like steel cables beneath his shirt. His voice was cold and biting. "A king's place is wherever he wills it to be. We're begging for a violent revolt if we fail to maintain our relationships, alliances, and treaties. My location is irrelevant—whether I'm in Hell's Kitchen or on the other side of the globe. If our enemies sense vulnerability, they'll come for us. Felicia's betrayal taught us that this compound is no longer an impregnable fort." Adrian spread his arm in a wide arc, encompassing the room.

He was haunted by the memory of Felicia's last words. They were like a snake's hiss, uttered with deliberation and a sense of urgency as she delivered her final message: Adrian's place in the world was in jeopardy, and those he thought he could trust were already plotting his downfall.

Her words had sent a chill down his spine as a snarl of secrets and whispers rippled through the air like a malicious wind.

Adrian remembered Felicia's laughter and sneering voice as she told him how narrow his scope of the world was, locked away in Hell's Kitchen. Although he felt a sharp pang of shame and embarrassment, he couldn't deny that her words held a measure of truth.

Adrian's mind raced. He tried to quell the dread and anxiety that crept in as he considered what might be waiting for him abroad. He shook his head, forcing himself to stay in the present and keep his emotions in check. He had to be strong and decisive, as was expected of a leader—expected of him. He steeled himself, squaring his shoulders and lifting his chin. It was the only path forward.

Kellan and Augustus remained quiet and didn't oppose Adrian's decision. He appreciated their modest support, but Adrian also respected that Royce offered a different perspective when he voiced his concerns. That was what separated his trusted adviser from the rest.

Royce, now composed, suggested, "Let me take care of it instead."

Adrian hesitated, considering the offer. Royce was not known for being a people person—in fact, he was hardly liked by anyone. His solemn manner and lack of social experience would be detrimental to the task at hand. Continuing down this route would lead to more broken bridges than repaired ones.

Adrian's gaze was steely and determined. "I appreciate that," he said, his voice firm and commanding. "But no, this is something I must do on my own. I remember the early days when I had to scrounge and scrape to make connections and build relationships. As king, I have a reputation that will make this task much easier."

Royce furrowed his brow, pursed his lips, and narrowed his eyes as he shook his head in resignation. Adrian took a deep breath and held up a palm to quell any potential dissent. "It is settled," he declared firmly.

Adrian felt the weight of urgency settle on his shoulders. He knew the stakes; it was dangerous, and he would need to remain vigilant to succeed. But try as he might, his thoughts were constantly interrupted by visions of a fiery-haired fae.

Once Adrian and Royce were by themselves, the vampire king braced himself for further counsel from his adviser.

Royce's face grew stern as he spoke. "You can't possibly be serious about your plan to venture out there. I suggest you think twice before you do something so foolish." He stared at Adrian with a blend of worry and censure, but his tone held a hint of admiration.

Adrian responded, "Perhaps it is foolish. But honestly, Royce, what else can we do? Ignoring our strategic relationships would be more perilous than me leaving."

Royce balked, as he often did whenever Adrian tried to explain his actions. "Forgive me, my king, but you seem to think you are invulnerable. You can be killed, and, plenty of people outside Hell's Kitchen would love to seize the throne for themselves.

Adrian fought to keep his expression neutral as Royce spoke, but his words threatened to trigger the memory of Felicia Lorne's vicious attack. He could still feel the wooden stake as it pierced his chest, and he knew if it hadn't been for Moira's quick actions, he wouldn't have survived. But still, he was determined to continue with his plan.

"Have a little faith," Adrian said, forcing a smile. "Won't you?"

Royce sighed sulkily, his thick fingers massaging the back of his neck as he closed his eyes. His brow furrowed, and he shook his head slowly. "You know I do," he said softly. "But I can never support this decision.

That was why Adrian had not shared his plans for this new venture with Royce. He would not be journeying alone into the dark unknown; instead, if everything went according to plan, he would have a companion. This ally would act as a bridge between the vampire seethe and the other supernatural creatures that Adrian needed to connect with.

But first, Moira Collins would have to agree to accompany him.

Thank you for reading the sneak peek into the next adventure with Moira and Adrian--Vampsire. It is available for preorder now on Amazon!

Please visit https://a.co/d/1jmW8nC to secure your copy!

Final words...

Thank you so much for reading Forbitten Fae! I hope you enjoyed getting to know Moira, Adrian, and the rest of the Hell's Kitchen crew!

I'm so excited to announce that Forbitten Fae is now available on Audible. Click here to order – https://www.audible.com/pd/Forbitten-Fae-Audiobook/B0BV9DRYY3

And last but not least––this is the part where I shamelessly beg! If reading Forbitten Fae gave you any bit of joy, please consider leaving a positive review on Amazon. It truly helps and I'd be extremely grateful! Thank you!

T.W. Pearce

Printed in Great Britain
by Amazon

19375356R00078